An Ellora's Cave Romantica Publication

www.ellorascave.com

Tempting Rever

ISBN 9781419964053
ALL RIGHTS RESERVED.
Tempting Rever Copyright © 2010 Laurann Dohner
Edited by Shannon Combs.
Cover art by Syneca.

Electronic book publication May 2010
Trade paperback publication 2011

LAURANN DOHNER

ZORN WARRIORS

Tempting REVER

ELLORA'S CAVE
ROMANTICA PUBLISHING

TEMPTING REVER

ജ

Chapter One

ಬ

Nine days had completely and totally changed her life forever. Brenda lifted her chin, staring up at the tall alien who was in control of her future, her heart pounding hard in her chest. She was a little afraid but mostly it was nerves. *What in the hell is going to happen to me now?*

Hyvin Berrr was the leader of an alien planet and looked to be in his late thirties but she knew he was much older than that. Defined muscles under deeply tan skin rippled with his movements as he paced in front of her, his body tense. He wore a shirt with loose pants that barely hid muscular thighs. She was on the planet Zorn and she'd traveled a long way from Earth to reach it.

Zorn males were all over six feet tall, mostly closer to six and a half feet, and they were big all over. He had broad shoulders, a thickly muscled body, and was very physically fit, making her believe they really were a warrior race. He stopped abruptly, turning to face her, and she stared into his beautiful eyes that expressed compassion as they fixed on Brenda.

"I am trying to be fair to you, human." He growled a little when he spoke in a soft tone. "My warrior who claimed you on your planet is dead now so you are without a male to protect you. His brother has been notified and he has a desire to claim you but he is a week from Zorn. As his brother's bound he has the right to take you into his home and he is on his way to come for you." He paused. "I am sorry for Valho's death."

Pain gripped her as memories flashed through her mind instantly at hearing that name. Brenda had a hell of a fight with Tim, her husband. She'd married the wrong guy but by the time she'd realized it, she was already in a domestic hell nightmare. She had spent four years trying to get out of a marriage on the slow road to utter misery but Tim had broken three restraining orders and finally had bullied her into being too afraid to leave him.

It wasn't a proud moment in Brenda's life to admit it was easier to put up with a man's shit, get pushed around, and be verbally abused than to live in the kind of terror she had when she'd left Tim. She'd realized after she'd filed the first restraining order that he was the type she read about from time to time, the guy who ended up killing the wife who left him and she hadn't wanted to end up dead.

Nine days ago they'd had a hell of a fight and Tim had lost his temper worse than normal, backhanding Brenda and ripping her shirt where he'd grabbed her, and she'd fled their home in terror for her life, just running into the nearby woods. She'd just needed to get away to think, to formulate some plan to get out of the mess she was in. She knew she was too good for Tim, too damn smart to end up staying with someone who was that bad, and felt ashamed that she'd let fear keep her in a hellish marriage. She was trapped, had no money to escape for a new life he couldn't find her in, and she'd been clueless about what to do to break free.

Valho had found her sitting on a fallen log wiping away her tears with the back of her hand. When the tall, long-haired man wearing black had suddenly appeared, terror had gripped Brenda hard. She stared up at the huge, muscled man thinking her life was over. His features were a little strange with his flatter, unusual nose and scary sharp vampire-like fangs revealed when he'd parted his full lips. He was scary big at six-foot-three with his bodybuilder frame and he had growled instead of spoken words. He'd held something out to her in his large hand at that point.

The fear had eased within a few minutes when the man's dark brown stare had fixed on hers calmly. She'd torn her gaze from his once she realized he wasn't going to rape her or attack her, seeing a small rounded object sitting in the palm of his hand. She'd studied it and then looked up into his calm expression once more, watching as he used his other hand to point at his own ear and then hers. From the gesture she realized he wanted her to put that round little thing in her ear, so she'd taken it cautiously, studying it more intently until she realized it looked similar to a small hearing aid.

Placing it in her ear had changed everything, the small object turned out to be a translator and she could now understand his growling. He'd told her how he was from a planet called Zorn, had come to Earth looking for a woman to bound to and he explained that bound was identical to marriage.

Valho had crouched down in front of her, talking to her, and she'd listened to him and made some decisions. He was really beautiful for a man, big, muscular, but so damn gentle, with the kindest eyes she'd ever seen. Their soft brown depths had made her feel safe, cared for, and three hours later she'd agreed to leave Earth with him. He'd made her a lot of promises, which she'd believed for some reason, and he'd kept them. He'd never hurt her, never frightened her, never...

She dragged her thoughts back to the present. Valho had been killed on the way to Zorn when the ship they'd been traveling on had been attacked by males from a neighboring planet called Collis. The whys were lost on Brenda and she didn't really give a damn since that wasn't going to change the fact that Valho was dead, her life on Earth was gone, and now her future was in the hands of the blue-eyed Zorn leader silently staring down at her.

"I wish I could order you returned to Earth," Hyvin Berrr said softly. "But as Valho should have informed you there is no going back now that you know of our existence. Your planet is not as advanced as we are, they don't have the ability to travel space like we do, but we don't wish war with your people if they have a problem with some of our males visiting Earth to find and bound with your females. Volder is a good warrior who will come to claim you. Did Valho say anything about his brother?"

Brenda shook her head. "No. He just said he had family and that he felt I would like them."

"Volder lives off world commanding one of our space patrol ships that protect Zorn from alien attacks. It is our way when something happens to one male for a relative to take in the woman." The man paused. "I told him that he would have to bound to you, which will assure that you will be well cared for and you will be treated with respect. We don't abuse our women."

Her heart squeezed in her chest. "So that's what is going to happen to me? Valho's brother is going to marry me? I don't even know him."

Compassion flared again in the electric blue eyes of the man facing her. "He will give you days to adjust to him before he touches your body to bound with you. You are in grief and it is our way to not rush a woman immediately. I give you my word he will be good to you, human." He paused. "You will have seven days to grieve your loss of Valho before his brother Volder reaches Zorn to take you into his protection."

She could just nod, knowing she didn't have a choice about her future. "All right. Am I going to stay here in your hospital where I'm being kept now until he comes to get me?"

At the shake of the man's head, he took a deep breath. "You are drawing the attention of a lot of males who wish to get a look at you. Human women are very attractive to our males and much desired. I have assigned you security guards but even they are a danger to you and I don't trust them to not attempt to touch you to appease their curiosity about your human body. One of my sons is going to take you into his home for the next week. You will be safe there under his protection until your future bound arrives."

Brenda nodded. "I understand."

"My son has his own human he bound to so have no worry that he will try to touch you." The man turned his head, nodding at one of the men assigned to guard Brenda. "Escort her safely to Argis Rever's home. He has been informed of the situation and is preparing a guestroom for the human until Volder arrives."

The guard gave a sharp nod. "Yes, Hyvin Berrr."

The tall Zorn leader gave Brenda a sad smile. "Be well, human. Your Volder will come for you very soon and he will assure your happiness."

Brenda watched the man leave the medical room she'd been living in for the past twenty-four hours since they'd arrived on the red planet. Her attention was directed to the guard named Kelir. He was nice enough but his eyes had a way of straying to her breasts when he spoke to her and his physical reaction to her was obvious if she were to glance down at the front of his black leather pants, a virtual walking hard-on around her.

"Pack your things," he softly growled at her. "We'll leave as soon as you are ready." He paused, his gaze running down her body again before he turned his back to her.

One of the Zorn women, a Zorn healer, had given Brenda some clothing, some personal items, and had given her a medical examination when she'd arrived on Zorn the morning before. She packed up those few belongings and walked toward the tall guard who turned his head, his interested gaze once again going down her body before he opened the door. He was physically attracted to her and didn't bother hiding it, but she was wishing that he'd try since he was making her uncomfortable. She followed him down a hallway, into an elevator and then they were walking outside.

The attention she got was frightening to Brenda when she saw a lot of big, black uniform-clad men stop to stare at her. She was starting to feel as if she were the main attraction of a show as she silently followed Kelir to a waiting vehicle that another guard was driving. The new man never once looked at

Brenda's face, instead his focus had totally gone to her body and a soft growl was the only sound he made when she'd climbed into the back of Zorn's version of a car.

Brenda took in the differences between Zorn and Earth as she stared out the window, noting the Zorn sky was similar to a sunset on Earth with its pinkish shade of light red during the day but no blue was present. The trees were black, red and purple in color. The grass just stunned her by being a dark red. Albeit strange, Zorn was beautiful and she couldn't ignore the appeal of the thickly wooded area.

"Why are we taking her to Argis Rever?" The driver finally spoke. "I was told that he already has a human of his own so why does he need two?"

Kelir sighed. "He is going to take her under his protection until her future bound arrives. She's being given to the brother of her fallen bound."

The man in front gave a sharp nod. "When will they become available to the rest of us?" He didn't sound happy. "Only the powerful have access to them and it is not right."

Kelir snorted. "Maybe in a few years we will get access to them but they are still rare."

Brenda nervously glanced between the two men. "What are you talking about?"

The guard sitting next to her turned his head, looking at her. "Earth women are very few on Zorn. Only Hyvin Berrr's family and some of the powerful families like your Valho have been allowed access to human women."

"Valho had a powerful family?" That surprised her. "He didn't say anything about that."

A snort came from the front. "He was a relation by pack to Hyvin Berrr and anyone in his family is powerful. Valho's father and Hyvin Berrr grew up together as best friends."

"So Valho and Hyvin Berrr aren't blood related?" She felt a little confused. "You just said they were a relation to each other."

"A relation by pack means associated with for a long time. Family is a blood bond that is shared," Kelir explained, his concentration fixing on her breasts in her loose shirt again, licking his lips. "Did you enjoy your bound's touch when he mounted you?"

The question shocked Brenda. She frowned, her eyes narrowing. "That was a rude question I refuse to answer and it's none of your business."

A muscle jerked in Kelir's jaw when he looked away to stare out the window to ignore her. That was fine with Brenda. She was irritated that he'd asked her such a personal question about her sex life. She swallowed, turning her full attention out the window again to look at the strange looking alien homes that resembled large, rounded buildings made out of some kind of stone.

Nerves hit Brenda when she saw the large, intimidating house they parked in front of where she was to stay in until Valho's brother came to pick her up in a week. She wondered if the male in this house would stare at her breasts too and make inappropriate remarks like the guards did. She hoped not, thinking it was bad enough being a stranger on an alien planet without having to feel as if she were a freak.

The front door opened and an older Zorn woman with flowing white hair down her back dressed in a long tunic-type shirt walked out. The smile on the woman's face was warmly welcoming. Brenda relaxed instantly as she exited the vehicle.

"Hello, human. Welcome to Argis Rever's home. He took his bound to the market to shop but he will return shortly." The woman held her hand open palm face up. "It is a pleasure to meet you, woman from Earth. I am Ali."

Brenda didn't correct the woman's odd handshake, just putting her hand in the woman's grip that Ali squeezed gently, keeping a smile in place.

"It's nice to meet you, Ali. I'm Brenda."

Ali gave a look to the men, releasing Brenda's hand. "Just hand me her belongings."

Brenda turned to watch Kelir get her bag, unable to miss that both men were staring at her body again, irritating her enough to make her clench her teeth. She didn't think she'd ever get used to being openly leered at by Zorn men who didn't even attempt to hide it or bother to apologize for it. To Brenda's surprise Ali snarled viciously at both men, imitating an animal, and yanked the bag away from the taller guard.

The Zorn woman shook her white hair as she led Brenda into a large living room. "Males only think with their mounting sticks." Ali carried Brenda's bag as she led her through the large living room and down a hallway. "I will show you the room you will sleep in. Are you fine? I don't scent fear on you but you know the female nose is not as sensitive as our males."

That surprised Brenda. "You can smell fear? For real? I didn't know that."

The older woman paused, turning around to tilt her head to study Brenda. "Our males have a very keen sense of smell. Didn't your bound tell you this?"

"Um…no. He mostly talked about how he'd take care of me, never hurt me and how he'd treat me with respect."

Ali looked grim as she turned back around, walking again. "I never met your bound but I am grieved for you. I've always been a house helper so I never had a bound of my own."

"Oh."

Ali paused again inside a bedroom, a curious expression on her face. "Do you know what a house helper is?"

"I assume you take care of the house? Maybe clean it? Do the cooking?"

Shock was obvious on the woman's features when she closed her mouth and then anger tightened her lips. "Your bound was remiss in his duties to inform you about Zorn males. The males are…" she paused. "They require sex often for their health to be well so Zorn men take in at least two house helpers if they are deemed deserving of having that privilege. Women are a reward on Zorn. It requires at least two females to satisfy a male's strong and frequent sexual needs but with humans it is different. Your bodies can take the sexual desires of one of our males without it causing you harm. Too much mounting with Zorn females causes painful swelling of their sex. Do you understand?"

Brenda was too shocked to speak but she managed to give a nod. Valho hadn't said a damn thing about this when he'd told her about his home world. He'd told her how it looked, how he'd treat her great, how she'd be pampered and taken care of, but never once said anything about his sex drive or about Zorn women.

"Our males who bound to humans don't require sex anymore from house helpers since your kind can be mounted many times in a day. I am old so I was assigned to Argis Rever's home days ago to clean, cook and be a companion to his bound. I will never be allowed into their bed." The woman sighed. "I wish it were not so. Argis Rever is very attractive and I overheard one of his house helpers' talking often about his sexual skill. I could have gone to another home but to live in an Argis house is a great privilege. I will miss the sex but I can always take care of that myself by meeting males in town for a sex encounter. Argis Rever won't mind if I do that away from his home since he's made it clear he will never touch anyone but his bound."

Brenda was still stunned.

Ali smiled. "Really, Argis Rever won't mind if I let a male mount me. When he informed me that he would never take me to his bed or come to mine I asked him how I was supposed to fill my needs to be mounted. He told me to find a male to gather with in town. I have never been allowed or encouraged to live in one man's home while touching another. It just isn't done but it strangely excites me to think about doing it."

"Okay," Brenda got out, shock still rolling through her and wondering what had she gotten herself into, deciding these people were a little nuts. "I'm glad that you're happy about getting to sleep with other men." She didn't know what else to say.

"Argis Rever won't touch you." Ali's eyes ran down Brenda's body. "You are delicate. How was sex with your male? Was he gentle enough to not harm your body?"

Taking a deep breath, Brenda relaxed. "I didn't have sex with Valho."

Shock hit Ali's face, her eyes going very wide with disbelief. "He never mounted you?"

"He was really a sweet guy who was very considerate of my feelings. All your men are really buff… uh… muscular and big. He knew I was a little afraid of his size so he wanted me to get to know him first so that I was comfortable with our relationship progressing to that level."

Ali was stunned still but she closed her mouth. "Was he killed right away? No male could be alone with you for long and not mount you. You are too attractive. Did he at least strip you down to examine you? I don't want to mount you but I have a strong urge to inspect you just out of curiosity to see what you look like."

Brenda just stared at the woman, completely speechless.

"There was a vid released of one of our males mounting a human. I did not see it but I was informed it highly aroused all Zorn males. It is rumored that your bodies are slightly different than mine. I don't suppose we could strip together and see the differences? I am not sexually drawn to you but I am just curious. The human my Argis bound to is not nice so I didn't ask her to see her body."

"I wouldn't be comfortable with that," Brenda blurted, shaking her head, and resisting the urge to back away from the tall woman, utterly stunned by the request.

Disappointment showed on Ali's features. "I understand."

A door slammed in the house followed seconds later by a loud snarl that made Brenda jump. Her head turned to the open bedroom door.

"Bite me, you big bastard," a woman yelled. "I was just flirting. What in the hell is your problem, Rever?"

A pained expression was on Ali's face as she moved for the doorway. "Not again."

"What?" Brenda followed the woman out of the bedroom.

Ali paused in the hallway, lowering her voice to a whisper. "Argis Rever is having trouble with his very difficult human."

"Don't walk away from me," a deep male voice growled deeply. "We are going to work through this difference. You are my bound and you won't purposely draw male attention to your body."

"I don't see your name tattooed on my ass, Rever. You're a great fuck but give me a damn break."

Brenda paused at the end of the hallway when Ali came to a stop, shock slamming through her at what she was overhearing. Peering around the taller Zorn woman, Brenda got her first look at a tall, red-headed human woman. She was wearing a long tunic dress that was tented on her too slender body and she was facing a large man with flowing black hair that was down to his waist. His back was to Brenda so she didn't get a look at his face.

A scary sounding growl tore from the man. "What does this term mean? What are you trying to communicate to me?"

The human woman put her hands on her hips, glaring up at the really tall man. "What don't you understand? You're a great lay and all but I'm not blind and your guys are fine, Rever. I'm talking super hot and I can flirt if I want. It's not like I'm going to go jump their bones. I get that we're like married or something so that wouldn't be cool."

The man growled again, the hands at his sides clenched into fists. "We are bound and you won't draw other male attention that way again, Tina. I almost had to fight four of them. You purposely turned them on and you enjoyed doing it. You tried to provoke a fight by bending over to make sure they saw your bared *unis*."

"Just say pussy or cunt. Stop calling it that foreign word, damn it. Would it kill you to say either of those two words? Yeah, I flashed them my goods and it was fun. Did you see that one guy fall over?" The woman grinned. "I thought he was going to come in his pants he was so revved up."

The big Zorn male snarled. "You admit then that you did it on purpose."

Tina shrugged her narrow shoulders, looking suddenly bored. Turning, she walked to the couch and threw herself down, just spreading her legs, revealing that she wasn't wearing panties. Brenda was shocked at the woman's behavior and with the view she displayed, flashing the man a beaver shot on purpose.

"You sure like looking at my cunt enough." Tina glared at him. "You sure like fucking me too. Why don't you shut up and do that? That should chill your ass out."

A roar tore from Rever. Brenda was so startled at the ear-splitting noise that she jumped back a step, completely expecting the man's temper to snap. If he hit the rude woman it wouldn't have surprised her but he didn't move. He just stood there breathing hard, his hands fisted at his sides.

"I don't want to touch you right now," he finally growled.

The outrageous woman looked furious as his words, her face twisting into an ugly expression. "For a guy who's a walking dick you sure don't want to fuck much."

"Go to our room. I am getting angry and I need to calm down. You test me, Tina."

"Oh, go fuck yourself." Tina stood up. "Don't be surprised though if I do fuck around on you. You're an asshole when you're not screwing me and absolutely useless except to piss me off."

"Don't ever, Tina. I mean it," the Zorn snarled. "If you let another male touch you I will kill him."

Snorting, the woman flipped him off over her shoulder as she strode down another hallway on the other side of the room, disappearing out of sight. Ali quickly advanced into the living room toward the enraged male. Brenda was too stunned over the argument she'd just witnessed to even think about moving. Ali rounded the angry large Zorn to stand before him and bowed her head.

"Argis Rever," she said softly. "Is there anything I can do?"

The man growled. "No. I don't understand her. She is nothing like my brother's bound human who is devoted to him and is sweet. This one..." He took a deep breath, pushing out air harshly. "I may have made a mistake and I don't know what to do about her, Ali. She tested my control on purpose by presenting herself to other males on the street. I think she wanted them to mount her, not caring if it caused me to have to fight to protect her. I think she wanted me to have to kill for her just for the entertainment of seeing a fight. I told her it would be to the death but she had no regard for their lives or my own."

Ali lowered her head a little more before glancing up. "The other human is here. You are so angry that you did not notice her scent." Ali's jerked her head in Brenda's direction.

Brenda saw the man's entire body stiffen as he slowly turned to face her. The ability to breathe right left her as she stared into a pair of gorgeous eyes that were the most beautiful things she'd ever seen—a bright, stunning blue framed by long, thick black eyelashes.

Argis Rever was a damn good-looking alien with finely chiseled features. His cheeks were strong and masculine, his nose was flat, wide and perfect on his face. Black hair fell over his broad shoulders and down his impressive chest, drawing her attention to the rest of his body. He was slightly bigger than Valho had been, his shoulders more impressive, with thicker biceps that were revealed in his tank top-style shirt, and he was a few inches taller too, probably six foot five.

He blinked a few times, staring at her silently as his full lips tightened into a firm line until that mouth parted as he took a deep breath. Tips of white sharp teeth were revealed a second before his lips pressed back together and his nostrils flared, inhaling sharply. When his lips parted again his tongue darted out, swiping a full, sexy lower lip. Brenda tore her focus away from his tongue.

The sexual attraction was instant and strong between them. Argis Rever was pure hot-blooded male. If Brenda thought Valho was attractive, she felt downright guilty at the knowledge that he was nothing compared to the man before her. A soft growl came from Rever a long minute later before he shook his head a little, swallowing hard enough that his throat moved with the action.

"Welcome to my home." He had a deep, terrific voice when he wasn't growling.

"It's nice to meet you," she got out softly. "Thank you for taking me in."

He took a step forward before he stopped, the lines of his body going tense again. "I knew Valho and I was grieved to hear of his death." He held out his large hand.

"Thank you. He seemed really nice and I liked him a lot." Brenda moved closer to shake his hand.

She realized she was staring at the large, sexy man but she couldn't stop herself from doing it. She felt her bare foot snag on something and suddenly she was pitching forward when she tripped. She would have landed face first on the floor but the big Zorn had super fast reflexes, launching himself at her to grab Brenda and yank her against his hard, long body to catch her.

Brenda stared up at him in wonder realizing he was that big yet that agile. Her hands were on his hot-skinned, muscular arms and her hold on him revealed he was really buff when her hands weren't able to encircle his biceps. She inhaled pure masculine male scent and he smelled really damn good to her. His body was large, fit and pressed tightly to her smaller, softer one as their gazes remained locked together.

His long hair tickled her cheek where it fell over his shoulder toward her but neither moved away. She couldn't tear her gaze from his knowing she'd never felt so attracted to a man before in her life. She wanted to slide her hands up his hot skin to wrap them around his neck and the urge to go on her tiptoes to tug his head down so their lips could touch was almost overwhelming. Her fingers itched to run through his long, thick mane of hair.

A soft growl came from the man, his nostrils flared again, sniffing at her, as his arms gripped her more securely and hugged her even tighter to his large frame. His incredible eyes expressed his shock and confusion over the instant attraction between them but desire sparked there too. She was sure he could see her own desire for him reflected in her gaze locked with his. Her stomach clenched and she felt warmth spread between her thighs, her body getting turned-on enough to react to him. It was as if a physical blow struck her when a sound made her realize they weren't alone in the room.

"Her warrior never mounted her," Ali said suddenly. "I don't know how he resisted bonding to her."

Shock tore through Brenda that the Zorn woman had just blurted it out that she'd never had sex with Valho and she felt her face heat with embarrassment. The Zorn man staring at Brenda with intense blue eyes tore his gaze away to give his attention to Ali.

Rever suddenly released Brenda very gently as if she were made of glass. He stepped back, completely withdrawing until they were no longer touching. His gaze slowly lowered down her body from her face to her bare toes and then back up until they were staring at each other again.

Argis Rever cleared his throat. "Why didn't you bound to Valho?"

Brenda swallowed hard to rid herself of the lump that had formed there, feeling shaken up inside by her instant attraction to the Zorn male. She'd never felt such an intensely sexual reaction to a man in her life. It was crazy weird but she couldn't discount what had happened since she admitted to herself that she still wanted to touch him. She had to mentally nudge herself to talk since he was waiting for an answer.

"I really liked him and he was nice enough to give me time to get to know him. We were spending a lot of time together but then the alarms went off and Valho rushed out of the room to go see what was happening. A few hours later a man came to our room to tell me that Valho had been killed by a Zorn enemy. I was told he died well in battle defending the ship that brought me here. After that they locked me in the room only bringing me food until we arrived here on Zorn."

Argis Rever was silently watching her until Ali broke the silence.

"I showed her to the guestroom and I am making her feel very welcome in your home. Are you hungry? Should I prepare food?"

"Hey, Rever!" Tina yelled from the back of the house. "Get your ass in here. I'm waiting!"

Rage twisted the handsome features of Argis Rever. He looked away from Brenda to glance at Ali with a jerk of his head.

"Please prepare food. Tina is being difficult more than usual."

"Of course, Argis. I am sorry for..." She sighed. "She is very difficult. That is the problem with aliens." Ali shot Brenda an apologetic smile. "You seem nice but that other one is not."

At a loss for words, Brenda didn't even try to speak. She watched Argis Rever turn quickly on his heel to storm away, heading for where Tina had disappeared. Ali sighed loudly when her sad gaze met Brenda's curious one.

"I won't give it many days until that woman does something really terrible. That one is serious trouble and she is going either run off with another male or drive my Argis to insanity."

Nodding, Brenda had to agree. Tina was being a real bitch. From the back of the house a door slammed hard enough to make Brenda flinch. The memory of a pair of gorgeous blue eyes haunted her.

Rever, of the planet Zorn, was the sexiest damn male she'd ever set eyes on. It was a shame that he was taken and that Valho's brother was coming to get her. If she could have Argis Rever she'd be one happy woman but it wasn't meant to be.

Chapter Two

❧

Brenda shoved the blankets off her body, sitting up, and thought no one could sleep through the loud shouting she heard coming from the other side of the house. The floor was cold on her feet when she got out of bed to go to the restroom, the noise only intensifying as she eased the bedroom door open.

"I don't care," Tina screamed. "Why don't you bring your house helpers back? I see why you jerks keep a few of them. What are you? A walking damn hard-on? Go to Ali."

Rever's response was unknown since the only one yelling was Tina. Brenda crossed the hallway to use the bathroom quickly and washed her face, guessing it had to be sometime near dawn. Rever and Tina had fought late last night and now they were at it again. If the big Zorn killed his human, Brenda was all for it. She was even tired of hearing the loudmouthed, annoying woman constantly ranting and she thought Argis Rever was a saint for keeping his temper in check.

Dinner had been a nightmare the night before with Tina's constant complaints about everything from the food to the things about the Zorn house she didn't like. Tina had completely ignored Brenda at the start of the meal until Rever had tried to start a polite conversation with her, then Tina had hit the roof.

"You want to fuck Brenda, right? You keep looking at her when you think she's not looking at you. I bet she's more your speed. She hasn't said two damn words since she sat down at the table and I bet she doesn't have the balls to stand up to a man."

Rever had growled. "Maybe she hasn't said anything yet because you won't be silent long enough to let anyone get a word spoken. You have complained since you walked into the room."

"I don't like this alien shit you call dinner," Tina had spat back.

Fury had tightened the man's features. "Tell me one thing you do like."

"Oh, screw yourself," Tina had snapped. "You're still pissed that I flirted with other guys. Just deal with it because that's how I roll."

A snarl had come from Rever as he glared at Tina.

"And stop doing that. You sound like a fucking dog and I told you what one of those are. If you walk on two legs then act like a damn man. Try being one for a change."

Rever was on his feet in a heartbeat, his chair crashed to the floor, breaking, as a vicious snarl tore from his throat. Brenda had felt fear instantly, thinking the man had finally lost his temper. Instead Rever had turned abruptly from the table to march away, leaving most of his meal untouched.

Ali stood up, grabbed his plate, and had rushed after him within seconds, leaving Brenda alone with Tina at the table.

Tina rolled her eyes. "He's got no sense of humor."

Brenda was pissed. "Are you trying to push every damn button he has? You're provoking him on purpose by totally insulting him."

Green eyes had narrowed as Tina glared across the table. "So what? The guy is a screwing machine but that's about the only thing he's good at. He's so much like an animal that I'm shocked he's housebroken and doesn't try to piss on my leg or hump it. He growls, for God's sake, like a damn pit bull. I love a great fuck and all but shit, he's horny all the damn time. The guy doesn't have an off switch unless he's pissed and then he sulks, being a big damn baby and won't touch me at all." Tina stood up. "I'm going to my room. The food here is fucking awful."

Brenda finished her meal alone until Ali returned looking pissed off. Sitting down hard, the Zorn woman shook her head.

"That red hair is driving my Argis Rever crazy. He wouldn't eat and is pacing the backyard trying to calm his rage. She has questioned his manhood. He is Argis. If she were a male he would kill her for that insult. Do all humans show no respect?"

"I can't stand that woman either, if it helps, and where I come from she wouldn't get away with acting that badly. It's just her. She's a bitch."

"What is that on your world? On Zorn it is a female animal that breeds."

"It's kind of the same but when you call a person that it's an insult."

A smile curved Ali's mouth. "She deserves an insult. If I called her a bitch would it upset her?"

"Her? Probably not. My guess is that she's used to that term and has heard it a lot in her lifetime."

"What would insult her?"

Hesitating, Brenda slowly smiled. "Tell her that she's an asshole."

A grin spread on Ali's face. "I know what an asshole is."

After dinner Brenda had talked with Ali for a bit before turning in for the night. She'd heard Tina yelling and she'd heard some snarls coming from Rever but after a while it had gotten quiet. That was until Tina's yelling had woken Brenda up near dawn. She jerked back to the present.

Brenda waved off the bathroom light and opened the door, stepping right into the hallway to return to bed. A second later she gasped when something large impacted with her hard enough to push the air from her lungs. She would have been thrown to the floor if two strong arms hadn't caught her, yanking her into something warm, fleshy and solid.

The light in the hallway was dim but there was enough glow for her to see by. She stared at a broad, naked chest in front of her face and two thick arms held her around her waist, knowing it was Rever without looking up at his face. She stared at a muscular chest inches from her nose, his skin hot to the touch, and she realized her palms were pressed flat against his lower stomach. Soft hair and hot skin were under her fingertips. Her gaze slowly rose to look at his face when he didn't release her.

Rever's eyes did glow in the dim light, the blue was amazing and that up close and personal, they were something she couldn't look away from when their gazes locked. Brenda wasn't even aware that she was still breathing until she noticed how he smelled wonderfully male and there was a hint of some kind of masculine soap, the combination an intoxicating aroma. He blinked at her and his arms around her eased the tight hold.

"Are you all right? Did I harm you? I was walking too fast and did not know you were going to step into my path."

She loved his voice when he spoke softly to her, that slight rumble gave her the best kind of chills. It was hard to think with his body pressed so close to hers, his warmth soaking into the front of her but she realized she had to answer his question.

"I'm fine. I'm also sorry," she got out. "I should have looked or something before I just stepped out."

"You had the right to assume no one would be roaming the house this early." His arms loosened even more but he didn't release her completely. "Are you sure I did not harm you? I heard you make a sharp noise and you are so little that I fear breaking you."

At five-foot-four, a hundred and fifty pounds, no one had called Brenda little in a long while. Rounded, sure. Curvy, definitely and even chunky were the words she'd heard to describe her body. Then again in Rever's arms she did feel almost tiny since the man was tall, wide, and just big all over. She still couldn't look away from him and she didn't want to, mesmerized by his gorgeous eyes. She could happily stare into those depths for hours at a time.

"I'm fine. You just knocked the air from me. Thanks for keeping me from sprawling on the floor."

He lowered his face a few inches to slowly inhale, breathing her in, and his blue eyes closed as a soft sound came from his throat that sounded real close to a whimper. The arms around her tensed, tightening for a second, before his eyes snapped open. He released her instantly, stepping two feet back so they were no longer touching.

"Are you all right? Did I hurt you?" Concern filled Brenda that maybe she'd injured him.

"I am fine."

"You have a pained expression."

Forcing her gaze from his, she let her attention wander down his body, realizing for the first time that he was damn near naked. She could only stare at his bared skin, her attention locked on a pair of shorts that looked to be a Zorn version of briefs, only tighter and form fitting on his hips, the tops of his thighs, and the front of them were presently tented, shocking her. The man was aroused and those shorts didn't hold him down. The fabric of them was thin and the outline of a thick cock was so clear that it left little to the imagination. She'd never seen Valho naked but it looked as though Zorn men were big all over judging by Rever.

An image flashed through Brenda's mind of her reaching out to touch him. The urge was there and she really wanted to trace her fingers over every inch of him. He smelled good and he was so attractive that she felt extremely turned-on just looking at him. She was having a sexually explicit thought, which wasn't typical of her since she didn't lust after men, but Rever was the exception.

Anger slowly burned in Brenda when she realized she couldn't follow through on touching the sexy Zorn in front of her even though he deserved better than that bitch Tina. He was worthy of someone nice, someone who had eyes and could see how handsome and attractive he was without hitting on other guys. She bet he was a great lover, remembering that Tina had said so even though the bitch had put him down.

"I apologize," his voice was deeper. "It is a reaction. Don't be afraid. You smell good and I am stimulated," he softly growled. "You are safe. I won't mount you."

She didn't look away from his tented shorts. "I wasn't afraid."

He inhaled, taking a deep, long breath that finally drew her attention from his erection. She realized he had shut his eyes again. He had an agonizing look on his handsome features. Blue eyes opened slowly, surprise flashed in his gaze as he stared down at her.

"You are aroused."

She felt embarrassment flood her. *He could smell that? Damn. That was unnerving.* "Sorry." She knew she should explain. "You're very attractive."

His incredible body tensed. "Do you think I am comparable to a dog?"

"No!"

He turned his head, looking down the darkened hallway toward the other side of the house. "What am I doing wrong? I anger her constantly and she insults me. She refuses to share a bed with me and she won't sleep in my arms." He turned his head back, those blue eyes of his fixing on Brenda's. "You are human. Please tell me how to make her happy."

"I don't know. She's not a nice person, Argis Rever."

"She was this difficult when I met her on Earth. She was kind to me at first so I keep hoping our cultural differences will pass but it is getting worse instead of better."

"I don't think anything you do will make her happy. Some women are just impossible to get along with."

A soft growl came from him. "Two of my brothers bound to humans and they are happy. What am I doing wrong? You are human so please instruct me on what would please her. I thought the sex would – that is the only thing that she does not complain about."

"I wish I had an answer to give you."

"Would I frighten you if I tried something?"

She shook her head. "What do you want to try?"

He took a step toward her but Brenda didn't back away, thinking whatever he wanted to try, she had to admit a healthy bit of curiosity for. A door opened, the sound making him freeze for a second, only his head turned to watch as Ali stepped naked into the hallway.

"I heard voices, Argis Rever." The Zorn woman ran her gaze over his magnificent body. "Has she kicked you out of your room again like she did last night?"

Rever growled softly. "She asked me to leave, yes. I was going to get something to eat."

Brenda blushed. Ali was bare-ass naked and seemed oblivious to her nude state. The big Zorn male also seemed to just accept a naked woman was talking to him without ogling her body. Ali had a nice, fit body that was a little muscular, and surprisingly firm for a woman of her years.

"That is not what you need." Ali softly growled. "You are highly aroused. I heard your bound tell you to use your house helper. Let me relieve your need, Argis." Ali moved forward, dropping to her knees of the floor, a soft growl coming from her throat as she crawled toward him. "Let me tongue you."

Brenda was shocked and could guess what tongue was. Her gaze flew from the woman crawling and went instantly to

Argis Rever. His eyes were shut and his body was tense. His hard-on was still pointing straight out—there was no missing something that size protruding from his body.

"I won't mount another," he rasped.

"You won't mount me," Ali whispered. "You are Argis and she mistreats you. You need release or you will get ill. You are bound and honored so you have no need to tend to your own needs anymore. Please let me do my duty, Argis. She does not care as long as she is not the one to touch you right now. Let me bring you calm."

The man moved and hit the wall with his back, shaking his head. "No." His eyes snapped open. "She might not care but I gave up other women."

Ali didn't back away, instead she kept advancing slowly, inching forward in a seductive way. Brenda was too stunned to do anything but watch as the woman reached for the man against the wall, lifting up her head to rub her face on the inside of his thigh. A soft growl tore from the large male while his cock jerked in response.

Ali softly growled back at him, running her fingers up his legs from his ankles to over his kneecaps, up his thighs, and to the waist of his undershorts. Fingers hooked in the material as Ali used her face to nuzzle his cock through his shorts. Another soft growl tore from the large man. He threw his head back, eyes shut tightly as his fingers clawed at the wall.

Brenda watched with wide eyes as Ali jerked his undershorts down. Zorn males had an unusually thick, rounded crown that reminded her of a mushroom because it was that much larger than the shaft, but his shaft widened an inch lower from the crown. She swallowed hard, stunned that a sexual act was about to be performed right in front of her. Argis Rever tried to turn away but Ali firmly gripped his cock with her hand, licking at the man as if he were milk she was lapping up, her tongue swiped up and then swiped up again just on the tip of his cock.

A groan tore from Argis Rever's throat, his hands flattening on the wall, as his breathing increased to a hard pant. Taking a step back, Brenda couldn't force herself to look away. She knew she should turn to flee into her room but she couldn't look away from the man's penis in Ali's hands while the woman continued to lick at him.

Brenda's body reacted to the sight of Argis Rever in the thralls of passion. The man arched his massive chest forward, his stomach muscles rippling, and a sheen of sweat beaded his beautiful body, full lips parting as another soft growl came from him. His hands clawed at the wall but then one of them moved. He cupped Ali's cheek tenderly, caressing her as she continued to lick at the crown of his cock.

Ali never put her mouth over him or took him between her lips but just used her tongue to swipe upward over and over. Brenda felt wetness pooling between her thighs when she managed another step backward. The man was the sexiest thing she'd ever seen and worse, she wished she were the one touching him. A flash of jealousy hit her and it stunned her. She barely knew the man so the emotion wasn't rational.

Taking another step back, Brenda bumped into the edge of her bedroom door frame. A jar of pain shot up her back in a flash as the edge caught her shoulder blade. Argis Rever's eyes flew open at the slight sound she must have made and those amazing blue eyes locked with Brenda's.

She watched his eyes narrow, his lips part, as he groaned deeply when he came hard a second later. Brenda tore her gaze from his to watch as Ali moved back to pump him with her hand, milking out every shot of release that left his body, hitting the Zorn woman's body. Ali used her other hand to rub it on her bared breasts while she softly purred at Rever. His body jerked with every stream of semen that erupted from him.

Brenda lifted her gaze to find Rever watching her still with hooded eyes. They glowed in the dim hallway right into her soul. She found the willpower then to spin around and stumble into her room, shutting the door softly behind her. Leaning back against the door, she realized she was trembling and really turned-on. Her nipples ached and she was soaking wet between her thighs. Shutting her eyes, she softly mouthed a curse. That had been damn sexy.

"Thank you," Rever said in a husky voice.

"My pleasure, Argis." Ali chuckled. "It is always a joy to please you."

Brenda could hear the exchange. She took slow, deep breaths, eavesdropping on the couple on the other side of her bedroom door.

"Is there anything else I can do? Do you want to sleep in my bed, Argis?"

"No. I think I will shower and eat."

"I could fix you something."

"You have done enough. Thank you, Ali," Rever gently dismissed the woman. "Please return to your room and get some sleep. It has been a trying day."

"Of course."

A good minute of silence passed until Brenda heard the sound of Ali's door firmly but softly shut. She relaxed, pushing away from the door and on shaky legs walked to her bed. The sound of someone entering her room made her gasp in surprise, spinning around.

Argis Rever stepped into her bedroom and paused at the doorway, dim light from the hallway silhouetting his body. His undershorts had been tugged up and his hard-on was gone now that Ali had taken care of it. Brenda raised her look from the front of the fabric barely covering him and blushed, discovering he was watching her and had noticed where on his body that she'd looked first.

"I apologize. Did we offend you? You looked upset."

Offended? That was the last description of what she was feeling that came to mind. She was confused, turned-on and suffering pangs of jealousy. She took a deep breath and forced herself to keep facing him even though she wanted to turn away. She didn't want to be this close to the man. He made her feel things that she couldn't understand, explain, and he was off limits to her no matter how much she wanted him.

"No. I am just not used to seeing other people…" She swallowed. "Sex is usually a private act where I come from. That's all. I didn't expect that."

The man tilted his head, his glowing blue eyes were fixed on her, studying her. He inhaled. "It aroused you."

Damn. She hated his keen sense of smell. Heat flushed her cheeks. It was embarrassing that he knew how much he turned her on. She kept her mouth shut since she didn't know what to say that wouldn't make the situation worse. Rever blinked a few times, watching her silently.

"Tomorrow I will take you shopping. Your future bound lives on a cruiser and you will need a hardy wardrobe. The least I can do after upsetting you is to provide one for you."

"That's not necessary."

"I insist. After breakfast be prepared to leave with me and I will take you to the village where we will take care of your needs."

The only need she had right now sure wasn't clothes. She was aroused and wanted a man that was in effect married. Brenda managed to not stare at his perfect body even though she wanted to look her fill since so much of him was revealed in those small shorts. She kept her gaze locked with his.

"Thank you. What time do you want to leave?"

"Be ready just after dawn."

"What do I wear? I mean, they only gave me these oversized shirts."

"That is fine. It is what our women wear."

"What about pants? Can I borrow a pair from Ali or from Tina? I don't feel right running around naked under my clothes."

A grin twisted his features, making him appear even more handsome. "It is the Zorn way. I will protect you so you have nothing to fear. You are safe with me, human."

"Please, call me Brenda."

He gave a nod. "And I insist that you drop the Argis and call me Rever. It is a Zorn title you don't need to bother with."

"Thank you."

The grin on his features widened. "After the hallway just now it seems appropriate to be on a first name basis."

A blush stained her cheeks. "Ali calls you Argis."

"She is a house helper and you are not. There is a difference. I will see you at breakfast. Good night, Brenda."

He left her room, softly shutting the door behind him, leaving Brenda to sink onto her bed. The man was flat out sexy. She shut her eyes. Watching Ali tongue the guy had been fucking hot. She just wished she'd gotten to touch him.

Shaking her head, she was shocked at herself. She knew it was out of character for her but then again, she'd never met a guy as special as the tall Zorn man. Rever just screamed sex appeal, putting all kinds of naughty thoughts in her head. Then there was the sympathy factor she had going for him to consider. He had hooked up to a cold piece of work named Tina and Brenda felt damn bad for the guy. He had no idea what kind of woman Tina was but she knew Tina was going to be nothing but heartache for the guy.

Chapter Three

ಬಿ

Brenda had expected a village market to be just the way it sounded, thinking she'd see a bunch of people with carts selling their merchandise. Instead it looked similar to a bunch of outdoor stores selling everything from produce to high-end gadgets that she couldn't begin to identify. There were more males than females, big men who dressed in uniforms or exercise wear. The women wore the long, loose tunics and seemed to shop together in groups.

Rever was dressed in a pair of leather pants that were identical to breeches from a pirate movie with a loose tank top barely covering his torso. His tan, muscular biceps kept drawing her attention as he walked her from vender to vender, touching things to show her. His head turned, those incredible eyes of his meeting hers, and he smiled. Her heart pounded every time he flashed that sexy look her way.

"Red would look good on you with your white hair. Do you like this color?"

Tearing her gaze from his, she studied what he was touching, a pair of pants resembling the ones he wore, only in a smaller size. A grin split her face as joy hit her. "Pants!"

He chuckled. "I noticed that you keep tugging at your dress often. Are you not comfortable bare beneath?"

"Not really. Every time there's a breeze, well, hell. I don't run around without panties."

He blinked. "What?"

"Panties are thin fabric that covers my, um, lower half. They are comparable to what you wore last night only smaller and form fitting to a woman. Earth women wear them under their clothes to keep their…um… private girl parts covered."

"Your pussy?"

She blushed a little more at this soft, husky tone for that part of her anatomy. "Yes."

"Tina said to call it that but your cheeks turned pink. Did I pronounce it correctly?"

"Yes, you did."

He nodded, turning his head to give his attention to the vender selling the clothing and made a hand motion. The vender nodded, wrapping the pants in a bag. Rever took her to a dozen more shops, picking out clothing for her, and then put everything together in a backpack he bought last. He shrugged it on his shoulders and gave Brenda a smile.

"Would you like to eat? I am in no hurry to return home just yet." His smile died. "My bound wished to come with us but after yesterday I refused her request because I don't want to kill someone today. Yesterday she exposed her pussy to males here. Doing that is an invitation for a male to mount her and I would have had to kill them if they'd tried. It was fortunate that they are aware of who I am so they backed off when I growled at them, realizing it would not be an easy battle to win. When she presented her pussy to them it was as if she told them she was unhappy as my woman and taunted them to challenge me to win her from me."

"Did you explain that to Tina?"

Anger tightened the man's features. "I did. She was amused."

Brenda's dislike of Tina rose to a new level of disgust. She'd heard the nasty woman going off early that morning but she hadn't put in an appearance at breakfast. It had kind of been a blessing. Brenda followed the large man down the street to a food vender. The smell of cooked meat made her stomach grumble since she'd just picked at her breakfast hours earlier. She loved Zorn food and it smelled delicious. Rever turned his head, a grin curving his lips.

"You are hungry."

"You heard that?"

He sat, motioning her to a chair. "I have good hearing."

She sat down, carefully tucking her long shirt tightly around her thighs. She noticed men around them at other tables staring at her but she tried hard to ignore them even though she felt watched. Her full attention stayed on Rever while he removed the backpack, putting it on the other side of his chair. In less than a minute a younger Zorn male walked up to the table nodding at Rever.

"Argis, it is an honor for you to let us serve you. What do you wish?"

Rever smiled at the younger teenager. "Give us two of your cook specials with large mugs of red *veral*."

"Of course, Argis." The teen ducked his head before fleeing inside.

"What is *veral*?"

Rever grinned. "It is a good drink but sip it slowly or it will make your head spin."

"That sounds similar to Earth's version of beer or wine."

He smiled at her. "How do you like Zorn?"

"So far I like it. It's a lot different from Earth but I'm adjusting."

His smile died. "I am sorry about Valho. He was a good warrior who would have made you happy as his bound."

She shifted in her seat and kept her eyes locked with his. "Do you know his brother, Volder?"

"I know him." Rever's voice deepened slightly. "He is not like Valho. Volder is older and keeps in the company of only his warriors on his ship while Valho was more social with many people of Zorn, rarely leaving planet. Volder is probably lonely for female attention so you will be good company for him."

"You don't like him?" She caught a tone in his voice that implied it.

"I don't dislike him but we are different. We are not friends."

Something in Brenda's gut tightened and dread spread throughout her. "Great. I'm to be given to this guy and I don't even know anything about him."

"He will care for you and you will be his bound and as such, it is his duty to assure your happiness. He would not be permitted to have a female if he was abusive. Females are a privilege in Zorn society. It is hard to explain but our history demands we protect our females and treat them well. If a male is found to be abusive he is stripped of the right to be responsible for them. At his age if there was a problem it would be known by now."

That was somewhat comforting. Brenda nodded. "Thanks. I'm just nervous because I don't know this guy at all and I'm going to be forced to marry him."

"It is our way. It will work out."

The teen returned carrying a large tray, setting down food and a drink in front of Rever first and then served Brenda. The boy didn't even glance at her as he bowed low to Rever and left quickly. Brenda watched him go, her attention returning to Rever.

"They all bow to you."

"My father leads Zorn. It is an issue of respect for my place in society and bowing to me in respect is my earned right."

"Should I bow to you?"

A chuckle escaped him. "No. You are not Zorn. Our customs are not known to you and I don't expect you to follow them. Eat. I want to get you home before the work day ends and the market floods with more males. You draw attention." His voice lowered, his gaze turned to intently study the tables around them. "They all watch you."

She couldn't stop herself from taking a look, confirming that almost every male at all the tables around them seemed to be staring at her. She blushed, dropping her head quickly, and reached for her food. They didn't use utensils so she ate with her fingers, mimicking Rever.

"I love this stuff." She pointed to the strips of red meat.

He chuckled. "You are a good eater."

She paused, looking at him. "I love food. You probably noticed that I'm a bit bigger than your Tina. She's way thin and I'm considered a little overweight on my planet."

"Overweight?"

"Not in good shape. I love to eat too much."

"You look very attractive. No male would complain. If I wasn't bound I would want you badly. Your body makes me want to touch you and explore how soft your skin is."

The thought of him doing that made her jerk her gaze up to his face. He refused to look back at her though, suddenly very intent on his food. He finished eating first and stood up.

"Let's get you home." He reached down, grabbing the backpack, and just held it in his hand.

Brenda pushed away from the table, giving him a nod. A sudden sound made her turn around to see what the cause of it was. In horror she watched as hundreds of bowling ball-sized creatures with thick, dark brown hair and big, sharp teeth came rushing down the street. It looked as though a stampede of the frightening looking creatures were headed right for Brenda and Rever.

Those things bumped into Zorn people down the street, some of the rounded, hairy balls of fur jumped a good three feet to hit Zorn bodies, snapping sharp teeth at their prey. Pure terror flashed through Brenda as it sank in that they were being attacked by vicious animals. A scream caught in her throat. On instinct she turned, throwing her body at Rever's, clutching at him.

Strong arms grabbed her. "It's all right," Rever rumbled. "They are just *Killis*."

"Kill us?" She squeaked, feeling panic seize her.

The damn things were flowing forward, spreading wider down the street as more of them came running from behind a building at the end of the street. They were rushing right at her and Rever still, attacking anyone in their path, their bodies jumping up and slamming into people. She spun, looking for a place to flee but there was nowhere to go except the chair she'd vacated. Without thinking she jumped up on it and turned to scramble onto the tabletop to get higher away from the ground where those horrible furry little bodies swarmed.

Rever growled, grabbing Brenda around her hips with one of his arms. He jerked her against his body tightly in a heartbeat. "Calm. It is safe."

She turned her head, watching the scary creatures all around them. They flooded the area around the table and chairs in the next second and one of them jumped, hit the side of the table she stood on and Brenda screamed. She was sure the terrifying creature was going to jump on the table and take a bite out of her with those sharp teeth. Another scream tore from her when one landed on the table with her and hit her leg, swearing she felt it tear into her flesh as the rough textured fur scraped her knee.

A snarl tore from Rever when he totally jerked her off the table, moving quickly, and held her against his chest. She felt her body pressed tight against his larger frame, blinded by his long hair when her face ended up buried in his neck and shoulder area. He moved quickly, running with her, to save her. Her arms ended up around his neck, clinging to him, and then he suddenly stopped. Her back hit a solid wall but it didn't hurt.

"Calm," Rever snarled. "You are safe and we are away from them."

Brenda lifted and turned her head but didn't release the tight hold she had on him around his neck. She peeked to see the street they'd been was now about half a block away. Furry round bodies were still flooding the street but they weren't rushing down the alleyway following them, the stampede staying far from them. She knew that Rever had saved her and gotten her out of the path of those things.

His arms were around her waist, holding her hip to hip with his body and she also realized her legs were wrapped around him. In her terror she literally had latched onto the man with her legs and her arms. He had her against a wall of a building with his arms around her, his big body pinning her there and he was breathing a little hard. She was almost nose to nose with him as she turned her head, their gazes locking together.

She stared into his gorgeous, amazing eyes. The color of them was so bright blue that she couldn't even think of anything to compare them to but almost glowing neon. They were striking.

Rever took a calming breath and when he spoke, his voice was a soft rumble. "They were just *killis*. They are harmless and not dangerous to you. They enjoy brushing against warm bodies but they don't bite or eat meat. They tend the vegetation in the cities. They are run through the streets to exercise them."

Brenda's heart was pounding. "What?"

"I should have warned you about them but I did not realize the time. You were in no danger. *Killis* are harmless. They run them in the streets twice a day to fuel their hunger for vegetation. They enjoy rubbing against our bodies and their teeth are sharp but they would never bite into flesh. *Killis* would lick you and massage their round bodies against your legs, being a very friendly species on our planet. Do you understand?"

She did. *Killis* were like little breathing Zorn lawn mowers that just looked terrifying to her alien self. A blush of embarrassment stained her cheeks as she realized that she'd flipped out over a harmless animal. She was locked around Rever's body, her heart pounding in her chest, and she was staring into his eyes.

"Oh. I saw them coming and saw their sharp teeth, thinking they were attacking."

A grin curved his lips. "I realized."

"It's not really funny. They are scary looking. It's those big sharp teeth. Their bodies look scary too, all round, hairy and ugly."

His chest rubbed against hers as he chuckled. "They are tiny."

"They have big damn teeth."

He chuckled again. "Are you well, Brenda? You still scent of terror."

She nodded. "I guess I should let you go."

He nodded. She eased her tight hold with her thighs around his waist where her legs were totally wrapped around his hips tightly. Her body slid a few inches down his and she suddenly gasped when her pussy came in contact with the front of Rever's pants, unable to miss the noticeable bulge there. The hands around her waist tensed as she stared into his eyes while he stared back at her. His grin faded.

"It is just a reaction due to you being in my arms. Even your terror scent arouses me. It makes me want to protect you and that makes me want to cover you." He cleared his throat. "That makes me think about mounting you."

The guy was so damn attractive and that hard bulge was pressed right against her clit, making her painfully aware of it. She bit her lip. Her breasts were smashed against his torso, his strong arms were holding her locked to him hip to hip, and her arms were wrapped around his neck. They couldn't get much closer unless they tried. The urge to kiss him was so strong she wondered what he'd do if she actually worked up the nerve.

"You should release me," he said softly. "We should return home."

Brenda moved a little, adjusting her hips against him, and fought a moan as her clit brushed that hard ridge of aroused Rever. Without panties his leather pants were an erotic sensation against her bared flesh. She didn't look away from his eyes, holding very still, just enjoying the moment. His nose flared as a soft growl tore from his throat.

She didn't release him as she battled with herself. She wanted to know how his mouth would feel against her own and she wondered how it would feel to be made love to by the man of her dreams. Rever was everything she'd ever wanted in a man. Kind, sexy, tender and they had more in common than he knew. Both of them had ended up married to verbally abusive people who just caused them grief.

Instinctively Brenda knew Rever would be a giving, incredible lover. The memory of his cock made her ache when she mentally pictured him working that thick length slowly inside her. The inner walls of her pussy twitched at just the idea of them together that intimately and she trembled with need.

"You have to let me go," he rasped. "I can smell you, Brenda." A soft growl sounded from him. "I am not happy with my bound and it makes me weak. It would be wrong if I took you here and now and your future bound would have a problem with it as well. You are under my protection."

"I'm sorry. I don't know why I react to you like this," she said honestly. "You just turn me on and I have the strongest urges to touch you. I've never felt this way about a man before, never reacted to someone the way I do with you."

"You aren't helping. That makes me want you more."

"Sorry." She shifted her hips again, rubbing against the front of him, and didn't even try to mute the soft moan she made. "Maybe it's this running around without panties but I'm really aware of myself down there. It just makes me more aware of how I react to you physically."

Rever's eyes narrowed. "You have need." He licked his lips. "I understand need."

She stared into his eyes. Yeah. She had need all right, she needed to be touched and her body was screaming for Rever to take her. He tore his gaze from hers, turning his head, to stare down the alley. It caused Brenda to follow his look as she glanced over his shoulder seeing that the little fur balls were gone. Rever's arms tightened and then he moved. He inched them deeper into the alley and around a building.

She realized there were no windows where he moved them. Two buildings narrowed into a vee shape with their roofs sliding downward to literally touch the ground. No one from the street could see them once he'd turned that corner. Her gaze flew to his to find him staring back at her.

"I'll ease you."

Ease her? She opened her mouth to ask him what he meant but then he moved his hips. He pinned her against the wall as the hard ridge of his cock rubbed against her clit. A gasp came from Brenda and her fingers tightened on his shoulders.

"Relax," he growled, moving his hips, rolling them, pressing against her clit in an erotic slow dance.

The moan that tore through her parted lips was something she couldn't hold back or even try to stifle. The man growled softly, his face lowering as his mouth went to her throat. He didn't kiss her, instead his nose brushed the line of her throat as he inhaled against her skin. His hips rocked, rubbing his cock back and forth against her clit. She felt wet need soaking the front of his leather pants, making their bodies rub together easier and pure ecstasy slammed her.

"You smell so tempting," he growled softly, his breath tickling her ear, his hot breath caressing her skin.

"Rever," she breathed.

"Come for me, little one."

"Please," she gasped out.

He froze, his hips stopping their slow torture of her swelling clit.

"Do you want me to stop?"

Swallowing hard, she pulled her face back to stare into his eyes until their gazes locked. "I want you inside me."

Incredible eyes narrowed as a growl tore from his parted lips. "I can't."

Frustration hit her. "You'll touch me but you won't enter me?"

"I am bound."

"But this is all right?" That didn't make sense to her.

"I am drawn to you in ways I have never wanted a woman before. I should not have touched you at all but I want to feel you come apart in my arms. If I can't have you I at least want to know the sound you make and the scent of your pleasure."

Their eyes were locked together. "Please?"

He growled, anger tightening his features. "Don't tempt me, Brenda. I made a mistake but I am bound to Tina no matter how I wish I were not. She could be carrying my offspring. If I enter you I know I am not strong enough to withdraw before I fill you with my seed and I can't bound to you. You are not mine to have and are promised to another."

Biting her lip, Brenda nodded. "You're a good man and you deserve better than Tina."

He growled, anger filling his features. In seconds he'd forced her away from his body. On shaky legs Brenda stood there alone, her body aching, her clit throbbing and her thighs soaked from wanting him. Rever turned away. He growled, taking steps from her before he stopped, keeping his back to her.

"We must go home. I should not have touched you but I enjoyed our time together too much and I smelled your need. I am sorry I lost my control but it won't happen again. I took advantage of your terror with the *killis*."

Shock tore through her. "You're going to take total responsibility for this and blame yourself? Let's be honest. The attraction between us was there the moment we met, at least it was for me, and we're both guilty of wanting each other."

He turned around slowly, his eyes narrowing. "We need to leave now. I don't trust myself and I am barely in control of my body. The need for you is so strong I feel pain to be with you."

Her eyes lowered down the front of his pants, the ridge of his cock very visibly outlined in leather. He was thick and long, rising up the front of his pants toward his hip. If he had the room between his skin and the waist of those pants he'd have been out the top of them. It didn't look comfortable for him to be trapped that tightly in leather.

Biting her lip, Brenda watched him. They were both hurting for each other but he wouldn't enter her. She only hesitated for a second before she lowered herself to the alley floor on her knees to look up at Rever, wetting her lips with her tongue.

"Come here."

Passion filled his beautiful eyes as he growled low in the back of his throat. It was the sexiest sound she'd ever heard in her life. He took a step and then another in her direction before he jerked to a halt.

"You don't know what you offer."

"I watched Ali do this. Let me ease you and then you can ease me since you won't enter me. We're both hurting for each other."

Rever only hesitated for a moment before he reached for the front of his pants and Brenda noticed that his hands were trembling as he tore open the front of them. He wasn't wearing undershorts today so his cock sprang free instantly. She swallowed at the sight of how damn big and thick he was, not sure she could take him in her mouth but she remembered that Ali hadn't even put him in her mouth, instead just licking him. He inched closer.

"Are you sure?" His voice was low and deep, more of a rumble than a tone.

Both of her hands reached for Rever, enclosing over a rock-hard cock. Her fingers encircled his very hot skin while she inhaled his male scent, drawing him closer to her mouth. She licked her lips again, inching nearer to the head of his shaft. Rever softly growled. One of his hands reached up to very gently caress her jawline.

"I have never wanted anyone to tongue me more. I have never felt this way before about anyone but you."

Her gaze rose to lock with his. She opened her mouth, letting her tongue slide out and surprise hit her when she ran her tongue along the slit opening at the tip of his sex. The taste of him was candy sweet. She licked more of the substance gathered there by his desire to make sure that first lick hadn't been wrong. Zorn pre-cum, at least Rever's, tasted really good.

Rever's body tensed and he softly growled at her again. She tore her attention from his passion-filled gaze to stare at his cock. Opening her lips wide, she took him into her mouth. Above her Rever gasped out and then snarled. It was loudly obvious within seconds by the sounds he made that he loved what she was doing to him as Brenda worked him in her mouth, using her tongue, her lips and her teeth to tease as much of him as she could handle while she sucked on him. She felt his body shake as animalistic sounds came from his throat while he panted and groaned.

Both his hands gripped her head, forcing her back suddenly. Her surprised gaze flew up to his, not understanding why he'd stopped her, knowing he was about to come.

"What are you doing?" He looked shocked and aroused at the same time.

She frowned. "Giving you pleasure."

His throat muscles worked as he swallowed hard. "You have to stop taking me into your mouth or I will spill my seed into you there. It feels too good for me to keep my control. Just lick me. I'm so close."

She frowned at him. "That's the point of me doing this. I want you to come."

He growled. "You don't understand. You will swallow my seed if you don't stop putting me in your mouth."

"I want to swallow you. You taste so damn good."

His eyes shut as his body trembled but he released her head. His hands went out to the building behind her, flattening there as Rever braced his body against the wall as he slightly bent forward with her between it and him. His gaze lowered as he nodded at her to proceed.

She wondered why he needed the wall to support him but didn't give it a second thought before she reached for Rever again. His cock was red and she saw how incredibly hard he was, knowing for sure he was right on the edge of coming. She licked her lips to wet them again before taking him in her mouth as deep as she could get him without choking. She moved on him, licking and taking more of his sweet taste.

She knew a second before he started to come by the way Rever shook all over. A soft whimper sound came from above her before he was exploding in her mouth. Warm shots of honey-flavored Rever filled her in burst after burst. She swallowed, moaning around his wonderful taste. He was so damn good that she regretted when he pulled away from her, forcing her to release his cock from her lips.

Her eyes opened as Rever softly growled. Her gaze flew up to his face, staring at him, noticing how flushed his features were and there was no mistaking the shocked astonishment in his eyes. More than that, she saw pleasure-induced awe. His gaze locked with hers while he hastily fastened his pants, covered again in leather in seconds.

Rever moved fast, surprising her when he yanked her off her knees, lifting her easily into his arms. Her feet left the ground and then her back hit something. She realized he'd put her on a slanted wall of the vee of the two buildings. His hand jerked up her shirt, baring her pussy to his eyes. He growled.

"Spread your thighs open now."

She only hesitated for a second before spreading her legs, wanting him to touch her any way that he would. She had nowhere to put her feet and from the angle of the slanted roof wall she started to slide down. Rever gripped her hips, lifting her back, and raised her higher on the angled surface of the roof.

"Put your heels on my shoulders."

She hesitated and then realized what he wanted her to do. She had to bend her legs to put her heels on his shoulders the way he'd indicated. It kept her from sliding in the crouched position he put her in on her back. Two large hands spread her thighs wider as a growl tore from Rever.

He spread her sex lips open with his fingers and without warning his hot mouth and tongue were all over her. She'd had men go down on her before but it had never been close to the way he did it. Rever didn't just lick at her clit. He used his aggressive tongue to slide the entire length of her, burying his tongue in her pussy first, wiggling it inside her.

Moaning, she gasped at the sudden and unexpected entry. He growled louder causing vibrations. His tongue withdrew, jerking from her wet depths.

"I want to fuck you so much I ache for it. My cock is jealous of my tongue. You are so damn soft, wet and warm and you taste so good."

"Please fuck me," she moaned.

Rever's mouth was on her again in a heartbeat with a snarl. This time he went right for her clit, pulling the small nub that his lips surrounded into his mouth, sucking on her in strong tugs, this tongue suddenly pushing hard against her bud, sliding furiously against the oversensitive bundle of nerves.

Brenda had nothing to hold onto so she clawed air and then finally the smooth surface of the slanted roof she was reclined on. Pleasure ripped through her as Rever unmercifully did things to her clit she'd never thought were possible and knew she wasn't going to last. She didn't have the ability to even try to stop the wonderful bliss his mouth was giving her. In a record fast time Brenda came hard, a cry tearing from her lips while her hips violently jerked under Rever's mouth until he pulled his face back.

She went limp when the last tremor passed through her and then became aware of her surroundings slowly. Rever was breathing really hard, her feet weren't on his shoulders anymore to stop her body from sliding down the building, and it was Rever's hand cupping her pussy holding her in place now where she was pinned on the slanted roof. She opened her eyes to see Rever's face was inches above hers, hovering there, looking turned-on with a wild look in his eyes.

"Tell me no." He growled the words at her in a deep, raspy voice.

Confused, she frowned. "To what?"

He looked down between their bodies, only about foot of space separating them. She followed the direction of what held his attention and shock hit her seeing that Rever's pants were torn open, his cock was hard and thick again, straight out and hovering inches above her pussy that he was gripping gently with his cupped hand over it. Her gaze flew up to meet his.

"Tell me no," he snarled again. "Tell me to back away from you, Brenda. You tempt me too much. You have cried out for me to fill you." He panted. "Tell me no or I will fill you with my seed. I can't bound to you and I know it's wrong but I want to still claim you. Tell me to get away because I have no control when it comes to you so I need you to refuse me. I would never take you by force."

She licked her lips. She tempted him? "Oh, to hell with it. Take me. Please? I'll beg if you want but take me. I just want you even if it's only this once, Rever. Please?"

Rever's eyes shut and he moved his hand away from her pussy. Her body started to slide down the roof again. She reached up, gripping his shoulders to stop from sliding to the ground about four feet from where she was. Rever's eyes jerked opened.

"Spread for me, spread wide and take me."

Rever's hands gripped her hips, lifting her higher so their hips lined up. Brenda didn't hesitate to follow his orders, spreading herself wider, lifting her legs to wrap around his hips that moved closer. His body was hot against her calves as she locked them around his leather-clad hips. He was so hard that he didn't need to guide himself to her.

A moan tore from Brenda as the thick head of his cock brushed the entrance of her pussy when he slowly pressed against her. She felt her body resist the thick intrusion but Rever pressed harder, albeit gently. Her body gave to the unyielding strength of the turned-on Zorn male with a rock-hard cock and he pushed into her body.

A moan tore from their lips as Rever filled Brenda, stretching her, causing pleasure for both of them. Her nails dug into his shoulders as she threw her head back letting out a loud moan of pure ecstasy.

"Yes. You feel so damn good," she cried out.

"Lord of the Moons," he groaned, sinking balls deep inside the tightest, hottest, softest part of pleasure he'd ever experienced. "You are the one for me."

She was experiencing those emotions too, the sense of being made for each other, and it made her think he was the one she'd waited for all of her life. Rever opened his eyes and so did Brenda, their gazes locking, staying that way, as Rever withdrew a few inches. He pushed forward slowly, stretching her and Brenda moaned loudly again in pure pleasure, assured that no one had ever made her feel the way he did.

"You are so tight and I don't want to hurt you but I want you so badly. I want to pound into you."

"Do it. I think I'm adjusted. Fuck, you're big but it feels so damn good. I assumed it might hurt but you don't go as deep as I thought you might. I feel stretched and full and every motion you make feels amazing. Fuck me, Rever. Please, just fuck me."

"I couldn't stop to save either of us right now." He started to move in deep, hard thrusts.

Brenda moaned, her legs locking around Rever's hips, clinging to just him since she didn't have anything else to hang onto. All she could do was feel as Rever totally controlled every movement their bodies made together. His powerful hips increased speed, slamming against her harder, and bliss tore through Brenda. She gasped, the climax hitting her by surprise and then she threw her face into his neck, screaming out from the intensity of how strongly she came. Inside she felt herself flooding with her release and muscles going into wild spasms as she came and came while he fucked her harder still.

Rever threw his head back, a roar tearing from his mouth and he started to jerk in tight movements against her. Inside Brenda she felt his cock pump, a strong heartbeat feeling inside her pussy and then he was coming. She could feel jet after jet of strong semen shooting inside her, his release almost violent, and then he suddenly collapsed on her.

They were locked together, both stunned, and both trying to catch their breath. She held him, wrapping her arms around him tightly, not even caring that his immense weight nearly crushing her made it hard for her to breathe. Dread hit her as reality sank in with the aftermath of their passion.

Brenda knew instinctively that as soon as she released Rever, he would withdraw not only from her body but from her emotionally. He was bound to that bitch Tina and he was a good man. He wouldn't just kick the bitch out even though Tina didn't deserve him, Rever was honorable.

He'd probably tear himself up over guilt of what he and Brenda had shared together in that alley. It almost broke her heart as pain sliced through her. Life wasn't fair and it hurt.

She wanted to be with Rever but he wasn't available to give her that option.

"I tried to pull out," he spoke softly against her neck, his voice sounding a little shaky and sad. "I filled you up but I could not stop myself. I knew it would be like this. I knew it." He shivered. "What have we done? What have I done?"

"Rever—"

"Don't try to take my burden of guilt. I am a warrior and yet I could not fight how much I want you." He growled, resting his face against her neck. "We must go to the medical center now. There is a shot you must take that will make sure I did not get you with offspring."

Shock hit her. "But—"

"No," he snarled against her neck. "I brought Tina here and I am stuck with her. Accidents happen and if you get a shot within an hour they can prevent my seed from taking root. We must go there to confess what I did so they give you the medicine."

Shutting her eyes, Brenda nodded but pain hit her hard. She wanted Rever, wanted more than she could ever have with him, and it hurt. She was falling in love with him and he wouldn't consider being with her.

Taking a deep breath, he slowly withdrew from her body, pulling away from her, and carefully eased her onto her feet. She felt wetness sliding down both of her thighs but she didn't have anything to clean up with. Rever moved back, pulling his pants closed and then reached for the forgotten backpack to yank out one of her new shirts, handing it to her, yet refusing to meet her eyes.

Her hands shook as she used the shirt to clean away the evidence of what they'd shared. Rever still refused to look at her as she righted her dress and he disposed of the shirt in a trashcan. He softly growled, bending to grip the backpack. He finally looked at her and the regret shining in his beautiful eyes about broke her heart.

"We need to do this, Brenda. They'll give you a shot and if there is a Lord of the Moons my family won't hear what I have done because it would cause shame that I lost my control. We need to go quickly. They will let us shower there so no one will know what happened between us when we get home. This can't ever happen again."

Blinking back tears, Brenda nodded. "Right."

Rever looked away, nodding. "I wish it could be otherwise." He paused, his gaze going anywhere but to her as the man stood there silently for long seconds. When he finally spoke again, it was so soft that she had to strain to hear his words.

"I am Argis and my place in Zorn society comes with a lot of responsibility but sometimes I wish it were not so. My father is the leader of Zorn and everything that I do reflects on my family. If it were just my honor I would lay it down to be with you always but it is not that way. I wish that it were because I have very strong emotions for you, Brenda. Always know that even if I can't be with you, I will always carry you in my thoughts."

Her heart twisted painfully. Her mouth opened but then she pressed her lips shut. What was there to say? They couldn't be together and it was tearing both of them up.

Rever cleared his throat. "We must go."

Silently, she followed the large man down the alley and back onto the street.

Chapter Four

ᔕ

"Where the hell have you been?" Tina was in the living room and looked really pissed off when they returned. "You were gone for five damn hours. When you took me shopping you didn't take me out that long. What did you do? Buy her everything on the damn street?"

"There was an accident," Rever said softly. "We were attacked by *killis*."

"Who the hell is that?" Tina frowned, studying Rever from head to foot and then Brenda. "She caused you to get into a damn fight? Did she flash her pussy too?"

Rever snarled. "No. Enough. It has been a rough day and I am hungry." He held out the backpack to Brenda. "Here are your clothes." He still refused to look at her.

Brenda took the strap of the bag. "Thank you."

He nodded, releasing his hold on the bag. "It was an honor."

Brenda fled before she broke down in tears, knowing he wasn't talking about taking her shopping, instead he was telling her that what happened between them really meant something to him as well. Before she reached the hallway she heard Tina.

"I was bored. I hope you had a good damn time getting into a damn fistfight. That bitch Ali wouldn't fix my meal until you returned. She—"

The rest of it Brenda didn't hear as she fled into her room and dropped the backpack, collapsing on her bed. A flinch hit her as her ass hit the bed reminding her that she was tender.

Rever hadn't been gentle when he'd fucked her and the shot the medical staff had put her ass still hurt.

Ali walked into the bedroom and studied Brenda silently. Brenda met curious dark brown eyes. Ali sniffed, her expression paled in her naturally tan face instantly, and then she reached over to shut the door, closing them both in the room.

"You've showered and you smell of soap but not the kind we have in the house."

Brenda stared at the woman saying nothing but feeling dread.

Ali sighed. "Something happened with Argis, did it not? I see the way he looks at you and I see the way you look at him. I saw it this morning at breakfast and I saw it last night in the hallway outside this room but I thought I imagined it." The woman's voice lowered. "He mounted you."

"Please," Brenda said softly. "Don't. Drop it."

Nodding, the Zorn silently watched Brenda. "Are you well? Is there anything I can do? I will never speak of this to anyone but it is my job to care for you as well while you are under Argis Rever's protection. What you say to me stays with me so if you wish to speak you may without fear I will share your words. I don't like his bound but I would never betray my Argis. To hurt his bound by letting her know he took your body with his would hurt him as well."

"How…" Brenda shut her mouth, frowning.

"How do I know?" Ali arched a white eyebrow. "I smell his release. I tasted it last night so I know the scent. You showered yet I still smell it so it means it is inside your body. He seeded you. Did they give you a shot to prevent it from taking root?"

"Yes. I won't get pregnant."

Nodding, the woman gave Brenda a sympathetic look. "He is a good warrior who has refused to mount me and I have tried hard to get him to. He must have strong feelings for you to fill you with his seed. Our men are trained to not release into the body of a woman unless they are so drawn to them that they can't resist. That means he wanted to bound with you but he is already taken so he can't keep you. I don't like the other human and I think you would make him happy. She does not. I could rid her of this house."

Shock tore through Brenda. "Are you offering to kill her?"

"Kill?" Ali paused. "I could."

"No." Brenda was horrified. "You can't even joke about that."

"I hate her for being mean to me and mean to Argis. She will be mean to you as well. One of Argis's friends stopped by and that asshole invited him in against my orders for her to not. She made me leave them alone to talk and that is disrespectful. I have good hearing and I purposely listened from the hallway. She offered her body to him but he left. He is a good friend to Argis who would never disrespect Argis but she still offered her body to another male. If I tell Argis he would have to kill his friend over that *coltorian* but it would rid us of her."

"What's a *coltorian*?"

A growl tore from Ali. "It means something very bad. It is a woman who gives her body to any male in need and she has no honor or respect for anyone else. They put women like that in medical buildings to let any ill man in need of release use their bodies. It is the worst thing a woman can become on Zorn."

"I got it. I think on my world your word means whore. You can't tell Rever what she did if it means he has to kill a friend to get rid of her. That would hurt him."

"She does not deserve Argis Rever. You can fight her for him. I will teach you how to fight if you wish and then you can challenge her to the death. He mounted you so you have the law on your side since he filled you with his seed."

"No. I'm not going to fight her." She was stunned.

"It is rare but we are a race with a brutal past. Women have fought and killed to gain powerful men. You could challenge her. I know Argis would not try to stop you if he thought about how he could be free of her."

"I'm not going to kill someone."

Disappointment hit Ali's features. "Oh. It is against your human code of honor to kill a rival?"

"I'm not a killer."

"That is too bad. I am not allowed to challenge her. The female asshole has demanded I prepare a meal for her so I'll go now."

Brenda watched Ali leave. She shut her eyes, relaxing on the bed, and the memory of Rever's touch made her shiver from wanting him again. The man could be addictive if she let him be. She opened her eyes and a wave of sadness filled her knowing that right at that moment he was with Tina. *Would he make love to her?* Jealousy and pain were two emotions that didn't sit well with Brenda but she felt both of them. Tina didn't deserve the wonderful kind of man Rever was and that pissed her off.

To distract herself she put away the clothes Rever had bought her. She smiled, remembering the fun they'd had together until the *killis* incident. She'd screamed over bowling-ball sized sheep with sharp teeth. It had been damn sweet the way that Rever had carried her away from them so quickly to calm her down.

She stopped moving, anger flashing through her, feeling helpless that she wanted Rever permanently. Gritting her teeth, she took a deep breath, letting it sink in that she wanted a man she couldn't have. She wanted to be his bound, she wanted Tina gone, but they were stuck. *Maybe the bitch would trade Rever for Volder.* Snorting, Brenda knew life couldn't be that perfect. Then again, Volder would definitely get the bad end of that deal since any man stuck with Tina would live to regret it.

She changed her clothes, putting on the red pants Rever had purchased for her with a thick, soft shirt that fell to her thighs. They didn't make tight shirts for women or ones that even fit properly. The Zorn women were bigger and taller than Brenda so the pants were a little baggy but not too loose. She left her room about ten minutes later heading for the kitchen to help Ali fix dinner.

Ali was setting the table, so wordlessly Brenda just pitched in and helped. Ali flashed a smile of thanks.

"The other one has never tried to help me. Much appreciated."

"No problem. Do you need help with anything else?"

"No. The food is prepared and I only made a light meal. Argis told me he ate earlier."

The memory of lunch alone with him, hours before, flashed through Brenda's mind. She nodded. She wondered how uncomfortable this meal was going to be.

She saw Rever first and he looked furious as he approached the dining room. His beautiful gaze locked with Brenda's before he looked away. When he stepped out of the hallway there was no missing the fuming Tina on his heels. The woman had her short red hair in a tight ponytail that stuck up on top of her head in an unflattering fashion but it matched the loose unflattering dress she wore as she stormed into the dining room.

"Finally," Tina groaned. "I'm so damn hungry I can probably choke this shit down."

A soft growl came from Rever. "Ali is a good cook."

"Then tell her to cook something good. The last two dinners were shit." Tina threw herself in a chair.

Everyone sat but Ali. She disappeared into the kitchen to return carrying two plates, serving Rever first and then Tina. Tina frowned deeply at Ali.

"Why do you always give him the food before me? Haven't you people heard of ladies first?"

Ali paused on her way to the kitchen to frown at Tina. "No. I have not. The males are always served first, then the bound, then the guests, and I eat last. It is the way that it is."

"I want served first from now on." Tina smirked at Ali. "That's an order."

"Argis is always served first. This is his home." Ali's frown deepened.

"It's mine too and I want served before him." Tina pouted, shooting Rever a dirty look. "Tell the servant to serve me first next time. I'm your wife and I demand you order her to do as I say."

Rever looked pissed as his mouth tightened into a grimace. "Ali, please serve Tina first if it matters so much to her."

Unhappily, Ali gave a jerk of her head but she looked pissed. Brenda clenched her own teeth together, feeling a healthy amount of anger herself. What in the hell was up with Tina? She purposely avoided looking at the woman. Rever cleared his throat.

"Tomorrow I return to work and I will be gone for five hours. Would you like to know what I do?"

"Not really," Tina used her finger to poke at a piece of meat. "Just don't wake me up if you leave early. I like my beauty sleep."

Brenda glanced at Rever, seeing his disappointed expression. She wondered what part of Tina's answer made him feel that way. Was it because the woman he bound to didn't care what he did for a living or was it because she didn't want to be woken up to say goodbye to him?

"I'd love to hear about it," Brenda said before she could stop herself.

Rever lifted his head, their gazes locking. His mouth softened. "I train younger males to fight."

"Wow. That's cool." Brenda smiled at him. "I know you're a warrior race. How old are the boys you teach? At what age does training start?"

A smile played at his sexy mouth. "At five. The males I teach are a bit older. I am an advanced combat trainer so the males I am assigned are between seventeen and twenty. The ones tomorrow have joined the Outlander crew that will patrol the areas outside the cities. Some of Zorn is still brutal. They —"

"Oh, stop already," Tina sighed. "She doesn't really give a damn. It's just polite conversation so stop rambling on. Nobody wants to hear it."

Anger darkened Rever's face. His lips pressed together into a tight white line. Ali walked into the room, almost slamming a plate on the table. She was a little gentler when she put Brenda's plate down. Brenda shot a dirty look in Tina's direction.

"Actually, I'd love to hear this because I'm very interested. I wasn't being polite."

Tina glared at Brenda. "Well, I don't want to hear it. It bores the shit out of me."

"Then don't listen," Brenda snapped, really pissed off now. "What would you know about being polite anyway? I don't care to hear you constantly bitch about everything but that doesn't shut you up, does it? Why don't you eat and let everyone else have a conversation that doesn't revolve around you making people miserable?"

"How dare you!" Tina stood up. "Get the fuck out of my house. I won't be spoken to that way."

Brenda stood up. "Someone should speak to you and tell you to get over your damn self."

"Females," Rever growled. "Enough."

"Tell her to get the fuck out," Tina snapped. "Now, Rever."

"I won't do that," he said softly. "She is a guest in our home until her future bound arrives to take her and I have given my word to protect her until he comes. It was an order from my father."

"I don't give a shit. I want her out." Tina crossed her arms over her chest, her green eyes glaring at Brenda. "Get the hell out."

Brenda was seriously pissed when she turned her head to meet Rever's tense expression. "If you want me to leave I can be returned to the medical center but first, do you mind if I have a little talk with your wife?"

He hesitated. "You will remain here but you may speak to her."

"I want her out now," Tina huffed. "Did you understand me, Rever? You get her the hell out or you can sleep on the damn couch for the next week while she's here. You sure as hell won't be climbing into my bed."

A snarl tore from Rever as he rose slowly to his feet, glaring at Tina. "Is that a threat? Right now I don't want to share a bed with you and the floor is preferable."

Fury hit Tina's face, making it appear red and splotchy. "You son of a bitch."

Rever growled.

"Stop sounding like a damn dog!" Tina glared at Rever. "Do we need to build you a damn doggy door and maybe put up a doghouse in the backyard? Act like—"

"Shut the fuck up," Brenda yelled, cutting Tina off. "What is wrong with you? You put our kind to shame. He's a good guy but you treat him like shit. Don't insult him by comparing him to a damn dog and especially knowing you upset him when you say cruel things. Ali is a sweet person, not a damn servant, and the food is delicious if you'd just stop being such a spoiled bitch and give it a chance. I can see why you left Earth. Nobody wanted you there, did they?"

Tina spun, a loud squeal tearing from her mouth and stormed away. Brenda went to move around the table to go after the woman but Rever suddenly reached out and took her arm, his large hand gripping her above the elbow gently. Their eyes locked.

"No. You won't attack her."

"Attack?" Shock rolled through Brenda.

Excitement laced Ali's voice. "Let her challenge her, Argis."

It hit Brenda then what they meant and she was horrified as she stared up at a frowning Rever who shook his head no. He thought she was going to physically attack Tina and so did Ali.

"I won't allow you to risk your life for me," he said very softly. "You don't know her as I do. She is very mean and has no honor. The fight would not be fair."

"I'm not going to challenge her. Is that what you think? I'm no killer. Someone needs to put her in her place. If you allow her to keep throwing these fits it's just going to get worse because every time you give into her she will just get more demanding. Do you understand? I have no intention of hitting her, no matter how much she might deserve someone popping her in the mouth. I just wanted to argue with her and hopefully make her see how wrong she is."

Rever took a deep breath, releasing her and retook his seat at the table. "No. Please sit and finish your meal. Let her go to our room to cool her temper down."

Brenda sat, hating the way Rever had said 'our room'. The idea of him sharing anything with Tina clawed at her inside where jealousy burned. The idea of him touching that bitch Tina just hurt. Her appetite was gone so she just stared at her food.

"Do you really want to know what I do?" Rever's voice was soft.

Lifting her chin, she stared into his beautiful eyes. "Yes."

The anger left his features. "Some of Zorn is still uncivilized. I am training males to patrol the Outlander areas to keep the peace and keep order. It is my job to make sure they are well prepared for anything they might face."

"Argis Rever is a well-known warrior who has killed many in battle." Ali smiled, looking proud. "He took over many of the Outlander areas and civilized them when he was a patrol leader."

"It sounds dangerous." Brenda felt a little fear for his safety. "Do you still do that? Go out there, I mean?"

Shaking his head, Rever resumed eating. "No. It is my job to train now that I am older." He didn't look happy about it.

"You aren't old. You don't look more than thirty-three."

He smiled, meeting her eyes. "That is old for an Outlander officer. They retire us in our late twenties to let the younger, faster warriors deal with the very aggressive. They make males like me trainers. I don't miss the harsh living conditions and I get to come home every night. While I was an officer and then a leader I would spend weeks in the Outlander areas living roughly."

Ali chuckled. "There are no women in the Outlander areas. Most of the males don't like working there because they have no females to mount."

That shocked Brenda. "None at all?"

"Not that we have ever come across." Rever sipped his drink. "Women would not survive for long out there without a very strong warrior male to defend her. The uncivilized males are brutal."

"The wild males would fight and kill each other over women," Ali softly said. "The women would be abused like in the old times of our history unless a family was strong and had many good fighters so they could protect the women from being stolen. The brutality stolen women would face gave them very short lives. Males would kill each other over the captured woman and she would be passed to the winner of each battle for her many times until her body couldn't take the stress anymore. We advanced but there are wild males in the

Outlander area who refused to change. Any woman out there would face that brutality."

"It sounds scary."

Rever nodded. "It is very dangerous. Your bound will never take you there so you will never see it or be in danger. Volder lives on the battle cruiser the *Drais*. We are not at war currently but we have had issues with a few other planets in recent years so the cruiser is out there more as a preventative measure."

"I don't think I would be happy living on a cruiser." Ali finished her dinner. "You will be the only female on a ship with a few hundred males."

That drew a frown from Rever. "She will be well protected and guarded. Don't frighten her."

"Sorry, Argis Rever." Ali lowered her head instantly. "That was not my intention. I know her bound will protect her. I meant she will be lonely with no other females."

Rever frowned. "Of course he will protect her and make sure she is happy." His attention turned to Brenda, their gazes locking. "He would not take you there if it was unsafe. You will be well cared for."

Dread hit Brenda at the mention of her future bound. What if she hated the guy? What if Volder was an asshole? Living on a ship in space didn't sound so great. She hadn't exactly enjoyed the trip to Zorn but then again, they'd been attacked and Valho had been killed. She didn't want to leave Rever knowing she'd never see him again.

"You will be well cared for," Rever repeated softly, trying to assure her. His expression softened. "He will cherish you."

She desperately wished it were Rever who would cherish her. She didn't say that aloud but she sure thought it as she nodded at him.

Rever tore his gaze from hers to look down at her food. "You have barely touched your meal. Eat."

"I'm not hungry." She forced a smile at Ali. "I had a big lunch. It was delicious though. Do you need help with dishes?"

Ali shook her head, standing up. "No. Sit with Argis Rever to keep him company." The Zorn woman collected the dishes and fled.

Brenda had a sinking suspicion that Ali had left them alone in the dining room on purpose. The second she was gone although, Rever was on his feet looking anywhere but at Brenda.

"I should go."

Her chin lifted so she could study his face. "You don't want to be alone with me, do you?"

Those amazing eyes met hers for the briefest second. "You tempt me. I must go."

He walked away without another word. Sighing loudly, Brenda stood up, feeling depressed, knowing that was how he was going to handle the attraction between them. He was going to avoid being alone with her.

Chapter Five

ഇ

"Tomorrow your bound should arrive." Ali carefully watched Brenda. "Are you nervous? I would be a little afraid since he is unknown to you. I have never gone to live with a stranger before. I always knew the few males I became house helpers to and was given the choice of living with them or not."

Biting her lip, Brenda pushed back her shoulder-length blonde hair. It was a hot day and her hair kept sticking to her skin. "I'm petrified. What if I hate Volder? What if he's an asshole? What if he's the total opposite of his brother? Valho was so damn sweet and he made me laugh."

"I wish that I could relieve your fears but I don't know this male."

"It's all right. I guess I'm going to get to know him really damn well since I have to bound with him."

"You are lucky to be bound. It is a great honor to be chosen to birth future Zorn."

Sighing, Brenda stared at her hands. Her heart was breaking but she didn't dare say why out loud, instead choosing to just talk about how she was feeling about Volder.

"What I am is terrified because I don't know this guy. What if I'm really unhappy?" She glanced at Ali. "Is divorce allowed?"

"What is this word?"

"Can I leave him if he's an asshole? What if he's abusive?"

"He is highly honored to have his position. He would never abuse a female and you must trust me on this. He will treat you well, Brenda. It is a matter of honor and he has much of it to be given the job he has. He will protect you and see to your needs and you will see to his. You will be happy."

What if I'm not? She wasn't happy right now. Brenda looked around the kitchen where she was seated at the table while Ali fixed dinner while Brenda kept her company. For the past five days Brenda had barely seen Rever since he'd gotten good at avoiding her except at dinner and those had been damn uncomfortable meals.

Tina was a mega bitch who took over all conversation at dinner, not letting anyone speak while she had gone on rants over stupid things, how the sky was a shade of red she hated or complained because on Zorn they didn't have television. Rever had eaten quickly every night before leaving the table. He was gone at breakfast, off to his job, and didn't return until dinner. After the meal he'd kept to the other side of the house, far away from Brenda.

It hurt Brenda to look at Rever. The memory of him touching her haunted her and just made her want to touch him. Her body ached for a man she couldn't ever be with again and the knowledge that he was sleeping with that bitch Tina just about killed her, never disliking anyone more. It wasn't just the fact that Tina had Rever, even though that would have been enough, but it was worse because she was such an unpleasant person.

"There you are." Tina stomped into the room. "I told you that I wanted you to wash my damn back and you never came, Ali." Tina wore a towel and nothing else. "I had to come looking for you."

Ali's mouth tightened into a line as fury burned in her brown eyes, glaring at Tina. "I am not going to do that and I already told you it is not my job. I fix meals, I keep house, I do the shopping and I serve general needs. Washing your backside like you are a child is not my place. I won't attend to a female's personal needs that way."

"You fuck men that support you for a living. Washing my back should be no problem."

Brenda went instantly angry at the implied insult toward Ali. "Don't you dare say those kinds of things to her or treat her that way."

Green eyes narrowed as Tina glared at Brenda. "You stay the hell out of this, you freeloader. If it were up to me you'd be living in a cardboard box. I bet the guy they are giving you to isn't really on some ship. I think he's hiding to avoid you as long as possible because he knows what a loser you are. He doesn't want his brother's used goods."

Standing up, Brenda glared at the slightly taller woman. "I'll wash your back."

Green eyes narrowed. "You'd try to drown me."

Brenda smiled coldly, her blue eyes narrowing as she glared at Tina, saying nothing.

"Ali," Tina snapped, jerking her attention from Brenda to glare at the other woman instead. "I want you in the bathroom right now, damn it. Otherwise I'll tell Rever you're being mean to me. I'll cry and I'll tell him that I want another house helper. You either get your large ass in the bathroom to do what I say or pack your shit."

A growl tore from Ali. "Fine."

Tina grinned coldly, turned on her heel and sauntered away.

Brenda shook with rage, deciding that Tina was the meanest bitch ever. She reached over to rub Ali's arm to comfort her.

"Why did you agree to do it? Do you honestly think that Rever will kick you out? I'll tell him how bad she is. He wouldn't get rid of me when she tried to make him and he won't get rid of you either."

"I know he won't make me leave but Argis told me to be extra agreeable to her, his reasoning is she will change if we keep being nice to her." A grin split Ali's lips. "I could accidentally hold her under the water until she has no breath left."

"I could accidentally go in there to help you."

Both of them laughed.

Ali sighed. "I wish I dared but I gave Argis my word when he ordered me to not get even for any of the mean things she does or says to me."

"I didn't make any promises but I was kidding. As tempting as it sounds to go shove her under the water, I couldn't really do it." Brenda chuckled. "Well, I wouldn't do it more than a few times but I'd make sure she could breathe between dunking her."

Ali smiled. "I am going to miss you. This is going to turn out badly for Argis. That human has been talking to one of the guards Argis leaves at the door to protect us. She is flirting with more than one of them and this morning when I went outside to remove the trash I saw her there laughing and touching one of them. When she saw me she pulled away but she should never put her hands on another male. Argis will be very angry if he finds out but I am afraid it will hurt him if I tell."

Dread hit Brenda. "Were they too friendly?"

"Not that I saw but Argis would have to kill the male if one took her up on her offer. She is his bound and the guards know it would be death. They are loyal to him but she still flirts. The asshole and Argis have not fought in days so I don't want to sadden him after he has hope that she will adjust to our way of life. If she is smart she will stop now that I saw what she was doing."

Brenda doubted Tina had a brain in her head but she held her silence, watching Ali leave the room, rising to her feet to stir the pot filled with a meat stew-like substance that smelled wonderful. Tomorrow she'd be leaving Rever forever when Volder arrived. Brenda's chest ached at the thought of life without Rever, knowing she'd miss his incredible eyes and the sound of his laugh. *Life is so damn unfair.*

A bell rang through the house. Turning off the flame, she walked out of the kitchen. Knowing Ali was busy, she went to the front door to answer it. Rever assigned at least four guards to protect the house while he was at work so if someone came to the door she knew it was safe to open it. It could even be one of the guards delivering something.

Four large Zorn males stood on the other side of the door as Brenda opened it wide. Their uniforms were black leather and they had weird hard-shell plating across their chests with strange designs in blood red by the shoulder. All four of them were brown haired with dark brown eyes. As she stared at the one closest to her, recognition hit instantly, seeing the uncanny resemblance to the man who had taken her from Earth.

Dark brown eyes similar to Valho's narrowed when Brenda stared up into them but unlike Valho, this man had a hard, cold look to him, and his eyes weren't kind. A scary, deep growl tore from his throat while his mouth tightened into a firm line before those lips parted to reveal sharp teeth. He snarled at her again, louder, making Brenda startle at the harsh noise.

"So you are the human." His furious gaze raked down her.

In shock, Brenda just stared up at the six-foot-three male, taking in the fact that he was big but not quite as big as Rever. Confusion hit her at seeing Volder a day earlier than expected and he was really angry with her for some reason. She'd been told he wanted to bound with her, that he was coming for her eagerly, but this man was obviously not excited to see her. He looked disgusted, put out and super pissed off.

Swallowing, Brenda forced herself to speak. "Volder?"

He curled his lip. "Who else would be here to collect you, human?"

'Human' sounded as if it were a sneer from his tone. A cold, dark gaze ran down her body again before the man turned his head, jerking a nod at one of the three big men with him.

"Get her things."

The man moved around Volder and literally pushed a stunned Brenda out of the doorway making her stumble back. The man walked into the house, sniffed loudly, and paused. Ali appeared from the other side of the house at that moment and Brenda met the other woman's stunned look.

"What is going on here? Who are you?" Ali moved forward quickly trying to reach Brenda.

Volder walked into the house. "Back off," he snarled. "I am here to collect the troublesome human. Show my officer to her room to get her things now, female."

Ali paled. "Troublesome? Are you Volder? You are not expected until tomorrow."

Volder snarled. "Do as you are told. Show him to her room to collect her things."

Ali jerked her alarmed look to Brenda but nodded. She still looked pale as she turned, glancing a little fearfully at Volder's man to lead him toward the back of the house on the kitchen side. Volder turned around, his angry gaze raking over Brenda again, definitely looking pissed off. Slowly, he circled around her, staring openly at her body with that enraged expression locked on his features.

"I had to stress the engines of my ship to reach you before you shamed my name more." He growled low a second before his hand shot out, gripping her arm painfully. "I want names, human, so tell them to me now."

Tears filled Brenda's eyes as she gasped. Volder was bruising her arm above her elbow. She stared up at the enraged Zorn man in his weird uniform with confusion and terror.

"I don't know what you're talking about. Shamed you how?" The hold on her arm hurt. "My name is Brenda. You don't have to call me human."

A deep snarl tore from his throat and the infuriated look in his eyes was terrifying. He jerked his head up and gave a sharp nod while he pushed her hard, knocking her back a few feet and nearly causing her to stumble.

"Hold her." Volder snarled the order.

A gasp was all Brenda got out before hands grabbed her from behind. She jerked her head around to stare up at the two men who each grabbed an arm on either side. Volder growled low, glaring as he turned his head to look around the room.

"The table."

The men literally yanked Brenda off her feet. She kicked air, shocked that the men had just jerked her up by her arms and as they carried her to the coffee table, Volder bent, using his arm to sweep everything off it, sending a glass vase flying to break on the floor. Brenda was swung in the air and a second later her back hit the table hard when they slammed her flat on it, facing up.

Shock kept her from trying to scream and the impact with the table had knocked the air from her lungs. The men who held her arms dropped to their knees to painfully press her arms flat on the table. Their other hands gripped her shoulders so she was pinned down on each side. Volder bent over her, rage almost poured off the man and all she could do was stare at him in stunned shock.

"I am going to kill every male you let mount you." He snarled. "Then I will punish you for shaming me. You could not wait the week for me? I have heard about your behavior." Both of his hands reached for her pants.

"I don't know what you're talking about!" Brenda was terrified, her back throbbing in pain from the almost brutal way they'd pinned her down.

A sharp tug at her waist caused her pain as Volder yanked hard on her pants, jerking them roughly down her legs. Brenda cried out in pain and terror, muffling the sound of the material being shredded. She tried to fight, kicking at

Volder, but he was too strong and fast, his men holding her down tighter until he'd completely ripped her pants from her body.

Volder gripped her legs in a brutal hold, pushing his weight down on them, forcing her legs to collapse until her bent knees were inches from her chest. A terrified scream tore from Brenda as the man pinned her so her knees were shoved even higher in the painfully awkward position. She felt air on her ass, thighs and everything else from her waist down that was bare.

"Hold still!" Volder roared.

Brenda stopped struggling because there was no point and she could barely breathe compressed in the uncomfortable position. Volder looked down at her exposed body, taking deep breaths, sniffing at her. Her heartbeat was painful as it pounded with terror in her chest realizing that he was now sniffing at her exposed ass and pussy and unable to look away from his enraged face, she saw when he frowned, some of the rage leaving his features.

"I don't smell any males on her." His cold eyes locked on her. "When was the last time you let a male mount you?"

"I don't know what you're talking about." She was almost sobbing.

Had Volder found out that I had sex with Rever? Would he try to kill him? Who had told this man about them? Only Ali had guessed—unless someone at the medical center had told Volder, but Rever had assured me that no one would. Her thoughts were racing.

Brenda trusted Ali and believed she wouldn't betray her. *Volder hadn't mentioned Rever so the informant must not have told him who had touched me. I'll die before I tell him it was Rever. He can kill me before I put Rever in danger.* Hot tears filled Brenda's eyes, knowing she was probably going to die as she mentally tried to prepare herself for the worst.

The sound of thundering footsteps made Brenda turn her head seeing three of Rever's guards rush into the house. They took in the scene of Volder hovering over her, his two men on their knees by her head holding her down and growled, reaching for their weapons.

"Back off," Volder ordered them.

One of Rever's men looked furious as he stepped forward. "Release the human."

Volder snarled. "She is my human and I am inspecting her. Get out."

A loud gasp broke the tense silence. "Brenda!"

Ali tried to rush to her aid but the man holding Brenda's bag suddenly grabbed Ali's arm, jerking her back to hold her in place. Ali turned, snarling at the man, and struggled in an attempt to jerk away from his hold, actually breaking free. She lunged forward again trying to get to Brenda but Volder's man lunged after her, grabbed Ali by the back of her neck and just jerked her against his body, to hold her there in place in front of him. Pain etched on Ali's face as she went on her tiptoes where the man forced her so she couldn't fight.

Volder growled. "We will take the human back to the ship." He glared down at Brenda. "Then you will confess to me the names of the males you let mount you while you shamed my name until I came for you. I will hunt down every one of them and they will die painfully for touching what is mine. Then you will be punished."

"I don't know what you're talking about," Brenda whispered. "Let me go."

"Release the human," one of Rever's guards ordered. "She is under Argis Rever's protection."

Volder snarled. "She is my human. Drop your weapons now."

"What is going on here?" A deep voice snarled from the doorway.

Brenda twisted her head, trying to see around one of Volder's men holding her, only to glimpse Rever. Fury hit his features a split second before a roar tore through the room. He moved out of her sight for seconds until he was throwing one of the men who held her down away from her, literally tossing the man across the room, sending him crashing into a table that shattered under the man's weight.

Volder released her, leaping backward out of the way of the enraged Rever. Brenda was released by the other man as he backed away, getting to his feet. She rolled off the table, falling off the other side, slamming hard on her knees in a crouch. She shoved down her shirt, trying frantically to cover her exposed girl parts, and watched Rever and Volder face off, rage etched on both men's faces.

"You came to attack my home?" Rever was snarling so badly it was hard to make out his words. Another roar tore from his throat. "How dare you."

Volder showed sharp teeth, growling. "I came to collect my human. I was not attacking your household, Argis."

Ali was suddenly beside Brenda, crouched next to her. She had grabbed a shirt from the bag of clothes and shoved the material over Brenda's exposed thighs. Shaking badly, Brenda gripped the fabric to hold it in place as hot tears spilled down her cheeks. She was in shock as she stared in terror at Rever and Volder realizing they were going to fight.

"I saw what you were doing. How dare you strip her and have males hold her down. What is wrong with you?" Rever snarled again, glaring into Volder's eyes. "What do you think you are doing? I should kill you for this."

Volder took a step back, sucked in a deep breath, and let his head lower until his gaze fell to Rever's chest. The man took another step back from Rever to distance himself and locked his hands behind his back.

"I apologize, Argis Rever. I am very angry and I meant no insult. I came to collect my future bound from your protection.

Thank you for keeping her safe for me." Volder glanced up at one of his men. "Get her. We're leaving."

Rever turned his head, glaring at the man who moved to grab Brenda. "Don't touch her." Rever's head snapped back around, focusing his attention again on Volder. "Explain your abuse now."

Volder snarled as his head jerked up to shoot a dirty look at Rever. "My abuse? You are supposed to protect my future bound but instead you allow her to shame my name." His head lowered as he took some deep breaths. "Thank you for housing the human but I will take her now and go. I know you are very busy and I don't blame you for her actions. As soon as I heard what she was doing to shame me I came as fast as my ship would allow."

Brenda watched Volder turn his attention on her, unable to mistake the anger and hatred that poured out of him all directed right at her. She shook with terror knowing that he probably wanted to kill her. Ali put her arms around her trying to comfort Brenda where she was crouched next to her, between the coffee table and the couch. Movement made Brenda tear her fearful look away from Volder and drew her attention to Rever who turned his head, his furious gaze locking on Brenda. She saw confusion there for an instant before Rever turned to Volder.

"Explain." Rever wasn't snarling anymore but his tone was furious. "What are you talking about? She has been a perfect guest in my home and she has caused no shame."

Volder looked up, glaring at Rever. "You are too busy to be aware of the human's actions but I have my reports. She will be dealt with after she confesses to her crimes, the males involved will be hunted down, and she will be punished appropriately but no serious harm will come to her. I would never abuse a woman but she will regret the shame she has caused me." Volder glared at Brenda. "I have given my word to bound to you as distasteful as that is but I will be the only male who mounts you while you breed my children. If you crave to touch males so much you will service my chosen few aboard my ship with your tongue." He almost spat the words. "Let us see how eager you are for other males once my men are done with you."

Rever roared. "NO!"

Volder backed up, shocked, staring wide-eyed at Rever. "This is no concern of yours, Argis Rever. I have come to collect it."

"It?" Rever was snarling again. "She is a woman. Get out of my home now."

Volder hesitated. "Fine." He jerked his head at one of his men. "Get her."

Rever moved, backing up to block Volder's men from reaching Brenda. "You are not taking her."

Volder gasped. "You can't stop me. I have come to collect the human that was my brother's bound and she belongs to me now by right."

"You are not taking her. She is not a house helper you can offer up to your males for her to tongue. She is not to be abused in any way." Rever's hands fisted at his side. "You come into my home, accuse her of crimes you have refused to state, and you had her held down while you attacked her. You will leave my home without her and she will remain here under my protection."

"She is mine." Volder raged. "You have no right to refuse me from leaving with her and you are overstepping your authority."

"You want authority?" Rever growled. "Ali, call Ral now and tell him to get here with his guards. He is the local judge so we will let him decide."

"He's your brother," Volder snarled. "I want someone else."

"He is the judge in matters of dispute and he will do whatever the law dictates in this situation."

Ali released Brenda, getting to her feet to run out of the room. Brenda huddled on the floor, gripping the shirt that was covering her bare lap, and shook with fear. If this judge guy agreed with Volder he was going to take her away. That concept sent pure terror flooding through her.

Ali returned in less than a minute gripping a blanket in her arms. She walked quickly, wrapping it around Brenda's body and she dropped to her knees on the floor next to her again.

"He is on his way. I did not explain since I have no idea what is going on," Ali sounded frightened. "He will be here in minutes."

Rever nodded, glaring at Volder.

"This is not fair," Volder growled at Rever. "She is mine."

"You abused her in my home while she was under my protection."

"I inspected her. It wasn't abuse."

"You had males hold her down while you exposed your future bound's body to other males and my guards." Another snarl tore from Rever. "You flaunt it to me what you intend to do to her when you get her to your ship and that would be abuse. Bound women are not shared with other males."

"They won't mount her but she can give them release. She is not worthy of being bound after she brought shame to my name."

"How?" Rever looked ready to hit the other man. "What are your charges? Tell me."

"Rever?"

Dread hit Brenda as Tina walked into the living room wearing a long tunic shirt to her knees. The woman was frowning, her arms crossed over her chest, and she looked pissed off.

"Go to our room," Rever ordered her.

"Oh, hell no." Tina walked farther into the living room, ignoring the guards and Volder's men to glare at Rever before turning her attention on Volder. "Are you here to collect her?"

"Yes." Volder turned his head, looking at Tina. "She is mine but Argis Rever is refusing to let me take the human."

"Damn it, Rever," Tina spun on him. "I want that bitch gone. Let this guy take her so we'll be rid of the freeloader. What is your problem?"

"Tina," Rever warned. "Stay out of this. I told you to go to our room."

Angry green eyes glittered. "I won't. I'm your wife and this guy is willing to take that rude bitch out of our home. What is your damn problem?"

Rever moved fast, gripping Tina's arm and spun her around. "Go to our room now. Do you see the tension? If a fight breaks out I want you safe."

Tina finally realized that Volder's men and Rever's were in a standoff. Rever released her, moving back between Brenda and Volder's men to protect her. Tina hesitated for a few seconds before fleeing the room.

"We will wait for the judge to get here and he will decide." Rever crossed his arms over his chest.

"He is your brother," Volder snapped. "That is not fair."

"Ral is a fair judge. Do you wish to insult an Argis?" Rever's black eyebrow arched, his eyes burned with rage, silently daring the other man to do just that.

Volder growled but didn't voice a protest again.

Chapter Six

ഇ

The man who walked into the room with four large Zorn security guards in black uniforms closely resembled Rever, looking angry as he silently observed the room. Brenda met his gaze as the man studied her for long seconds, sniffed the air, his eyes narrowing on her, took notice of Ali crouching next to her, and finally turned his full attention on Rever.

"What is going on?" His voice even sounded very similar to Rever's.

"Argis Rever is refusing to allow me to take my promised bound human, Argis Ral." Volder had calmed enough to not snarl.

"He has accused her of shaming him," Rever growled, obviously still pissed off. "I walked into my home to see him and two of his men holding her down, Ral. They had stripped her bare from the waist down exposing her body to their view. He informed me that he is going to share her with his men when he takes her to his ship."

The big Zorn named Ral visibly paled in shock as his bright blue eyes narrowed on Volder. "Is this true? She is human. I am aware that Valho bound to her and that he died. We are sorry for your loss. Valho was a well-respected friend of mine. I was told you had accepted a bounding agreement to this woman and know that she is no house helper. You won't share her with other males."

"She has shamed my name."

"How?" Rever took a menacing step forward. "He keeps saying that but he has refused to state why he believes it."

Straightening his shoulders, Volder glared at Rever. "I have reports of her behavior, of exposing her body to males and she has let many of them mount her."

"That is not true," Rever snarled. "What reports? Ali? Stand up now. You have spent all your time with Brenda. Tell him the truth."

Ali got up slowly to her feet looking frightened. "That is not true, Volder. Brenda only left the house once and that was when Argis Rever took her shopping. She has had no other contact with males except for Argis Rever. She has not even spoken to the guards."

A frown marred Volder's features. "I have my reports."

"Who told you this?" Rever inched closer, looking furious.

Volder swallowed. "It was your own bound, Argis Rever. Your human contacted me on my ship to tell me that my human was behaving this way and your bound stated she witnessed males mounting my future bound in the backyard of your home when you were not present to prevent it. Your bound did not want to shame you by telling you so she contacted me to come get my human before word got out that caused shame to us both."

Shock tore through the room. Brenda had the urge to kill a tall, slim, lying red headed bitch who had told Volder a bunch of bullshit lies.

"TINA!" Rever roared her name.

In minutes a pale Tina walked out of the hallway with her arms crossed over her breasts, looking nervous. "Yes? You shouted?"

Rever hesitated before slowly stalking toward her. "You contacted Volder on his ship? You lied to him?"

She shook her head. "I have no idea what you're talking about."

Volder gasped. "It was her on the vid. She is the one I spoke to."

Rever's entire body shivered a little as he glared at Tina. "Tell me the truth."

"I have no idea what he's talking about." Tina stuck her chin up, glaring at Rever.

"She did contact me on the vid," Volder growled. "Check your logs. Those vids came from your home and she contacted me twice to tell me that the human was being mounted by many males and that my human was causing shame to both of us since she was behaving badly in the home of an Argis."

Ral cleared his throat. "It seems someone is lying."

Rever growled, glaring at Tina. "Not someone. Explain yourself now, Tina. This is not a game. This is serious."

"Well, when you wouldn't get her the hell out of here, I contacted that guy." She pointed at Volder. "And he was in no damn hurry to come get her so I figured if I told him she was fucking anything that moved he'd hurry his ass up. That bitch is rude to me, Rever. This is my damn house and you wouldn't get her the hell out so this is really your fault for making me do something that drastic."

Rever spun away. He was breathing hard as he walked to a wall, facing it, and took more deep breaths. Rage almost poured off him.

"So the human lied to me?" Volder growled. "My future bound did not shame me?"

Ral looked pissed. "It appears she did not. It appears that my brother has bound to an *ovolion*."

"What in the hell did you just call me?" Tina glared at Ral. "And who the fuck do you think you are to look at me like that?"

"An *ovolion*," Rever growled, turning back around, "is a person without honor who tells lies to make trouble for all around them. They are the worst of society." He snarled. "Go to our room now."

"Fuck yourself." Tina glared at him. "Don't tell me what to do and don't talk to me in that tone ever again."

Rever roared, taking two steps at Tina, looking enraged. She screamed, spun around, and ran down the hallway toward the bedroom. He was shaking and he took heavy breaths as he stopped. Ral hesitated a second before walking up to Rever's side to place a large hand on his brother's shoulder.

"Calm."

"She lied."

"I know." Ral sighed. "I can't imagine what you are going through right now but you need to calm. She is a woman and she is your bound."

Rever's head fell forward and his shoulders sagged, not moving or speaking. He looked broken to Brenda and it tore at her heart. He was such a good man and Tina had betrayed him in just one more way. Zorn males were proud and honest so Rever had to be feeling ashamed of Tina and her actions. It had to be extra humiliating that this had happened in front of other men on top of it all.

"I will take the human now," Volder said softly. "Obviously I was misinformed."

Rever's head snapped up as terror hit Brenda. She didn't want to go with Volder. The guy was an asshole who hadn't even given her a chance to defend the accusations against her, just assumed instant guilt on her part. He'd attacked her, had his men hold her down, bruise her up probably from the hard slam on the table, and had torn off her pants. He'd threatened to punish her by sharing her with his men and to add insult to injury, he'd called her an 'it'. She didn't want to go anywhere with the creep.

Rage burned in his bright blue eyes as Rever slowly turned. "You won't take her from my home."

Brenda felt gratitude flood her. "Thank God."

Volder frowned. "You can't stop me from taking what is mine already. She has been cleared of the crimes and is in no need of your protection any longer now that she won't be punished."

Rever's attention turned to Brenda, rage still showing in his eyes as their gazes locked together. "Do you wish to bound with him?"

"No," she shook her head. "Please don't let Volder take me. I don't want anything to do with him."

He gave her a sharp nod, shifting his focus off her, his expression hardening as he glared at Volder. "She stays with me."

"Rever," Ral said softly. "She is promised to him."

"Scent her terror," Rever growled. "He was going to share her with his men and he attacked her without giving her a chance to defend herself against the charges. He walked in here assuming she was guilty, he let her be touched by his men, and forced her stripped bare in front of other males. She won't leave my house. I extend my protection to her." Rever glared at his brother.

Ral took a deep breath, staring at his brother, and then gave his full attention to Volder. "Perhaps you should leave to let things settle down. The human does scent terror and Rever is protective of her since she has been under his roof in his care. Go for a few hours, let the tension subside and then you can collect her."

"My ship is waiting and I want her now." Volder was angry.

Ral moved toward the man. "Let us go have a drink and eat a meal together. You have Rever on edge and need to let things calm before you collect her. As Argis I insist."

Looking anything but happy, Volder nodded, turning to Brenda. "Prepare yourself to leave this house in a few hours. You are mine and I am taking you back to my ship with me."

Brenda stared at Volder in horror, frozen. Ral took all the guards, Volder, and Volder's men with him when he exited the room. When the front door shut loudly Ali moved first, closing the distance between herself and Brenda to rub her in a comforting gesture when she went to her knees again.

"Are you well? Did they hurt you? I scent blood on you."

"Blood?" Brenda was surprised. Her back hurt a little and her elbow and she knew she was in shock but she didn't know she was bleeding. "Are you sure?"

A soft growl sounded. "Move, Ali. You go secure Tina in my room and keep her in place even if you have to physically restrain her. She is to not leave, understood? I will tend to Brenda. Go guard that *ovolion*," he snarled.

Brenda looked up at Rever as Ali got to her feet to run out of the room toward the back of the house. Rever looked pale as he crouched down. His nostrils flared as he sniffed at her, their gazes locking together, and she couldn't miss the anger she saw in his beautiful eyes. He held out his arms to her.

"Come to me."

He didn't have to say it twice. Hot tears filled Brenda's eyes as she almost threw herself at him. Two strong arms wrapped around her body, blanket and all, and then Rever was lifting her, to gently cradle her in his hold while he walked to her side of the house. She turned, burying her head in his shirt and let the tears fall, knowing she'd never been so terrified in her life and Volder was coming back for her.

"I have you, Brenda." Rever's voice was husky.

"Please don't make me leave with him."

His arms tightened. "I smell blood on you. Where did they hurt you?"

"I don't know. My back hurts. They slammed me pretty hard on the table."

Rever walked them into the bathroom where he gently shifted her in his arms and placed her on the edge of the counter. She looked up at him, meeting his concerned look. He reached for the blanket to tug it away from her body.

Her thighs were exposed and the shirt she had on barely covered her lap. Rever pushed the blanket completely away from her, letting it fall to the floor. He turned his attention from Brenda's face as he reached for her waist, his hands gently gripping her hips.

"I would never hurt you. You scent so strongly of fear."

"I'm not afraid of you." She meant it.

As their gazes locked together his mouth parted as his tongue slid out, running over his lower lip, and the urge to kiss him hit Brenda hard. She wanted desperately to experience those lips against hers and longed to know if his mouth was as inviting as it appeared. A soft growl came from Rever.

"Don't look at me like that."

She stared into his beautiful eyes. "I can't help it. When I look at you, I want to touch you and I want you to touch me back."

He broke eye contact. "I am bound to her and I'm trapped, Brenda. I wish it were not so but I can't be unbound to a human. It is for their protection and it was part of the agreement I made when I took one from Earth."

Pain lanced through Brenda. "I really don't give a damn about her protection after what she did to all of us. If you hadn't arrived when you did, Volder would have taken me out of here and I have a real good idea what kind of future I would have had if he thought all those lies had been true. She put Ali in danger because she tried to protect me and one of those jerks had Ali by her throat. Tina lied and I know it made you feel really bad to have her behave that way in front of those men."

"I know." His fingers gripped her shirt, his hands brushing her waist through the thin material. "Let me take this off you to find where you are injured."

She lifted her arms as Rever tugged her shirt up her body, leaving her naked, sitting on the counter. She couldn't look away from Rever's eyes as the man slowly caressed her body with his gaze. She saw longing in his face, desire, and she had no doubt what he was thinking because she was thinking the same thing. He wanted her as much as she wanted him and he couldn't hide that from her, not that he tried to mask it. Another soft growl rumbled from his throat as their eyes met.

"I don't want to leave you. Please let me stay here with you. Don't let that man take me away."

His eyes closed, his massive chest expanded as he took a deep breath but then his beautiful blue eyes opened. "I wish you were, Brenda, but you are not mine to keep. You have no idea how much I wish I could claim you. When I saw those males touching you and scented your terror I wanted to kill every one of them." His hand lifted to gently cup her cheek in his large, warm hand. "If I did not have a bound I would challenge Volder to the death for you."

Shock tore through her. "To the death?"

"You belong to him according to the laws. You were bound to his brother so when Valho died it became Volder's right to claim you and he did so by agreeing to come get you. The only way to take a female from a male who has claimed her is to challenge him to the death with her permission. Upon challenge a male will either release his claim or he will fight to keep her but I have no lawful right to challenge him since I'm bound already." Rever looked tortured. "I have to let him take you but I don't want to. The law is on his side in this matter and I have no way to fight his claim. The only reason you are still here is because I knew my brother would force Volder to state his accusations and I wanted Ral to witness the abuse so he'd have reason to prevent Volder from taking you. I know Ral is angry at your treatment but Volder has promised to not abuse you so Ral has to follow the law. Neither one of us can stop Volder now."

Hot tears filled Brenda's eyes, blinding her. She looked away from him to stare at his broad chest that looked tempting to snuggle into. She knew how it felt to be held by him and she wanted to always know that feeling. His hand left her face when he moved.

"Turn for me and let me see where you are hurt."

She shifted on the counter, sitting sideways to give him access to her back. She blinked away her tears before looking at him again to see that he was staring at her lower back with a furious look on his face. He moved, his chest brushing against her shoulder and arm as he turned on the faucet. Water sounded in the bathroom.

His bare hand used the cool water to wipe at her hip. She twisted her head to try to see where he was touching her but couldn't see it so she watched his face instead. His concentration was fixed on washing her with his hand.

"You were scratched but it is not deep." His mouth pressed into a tight line for a second as he swallowed. "Volder got you with his fingernail when he attacked you."

"He tore my pants off."

Rever took a deep breath while his hand paused on her skin before resuming his light cleansing. The cool water felt good and took away the slight burning sensation the injury had caused her. Rever's hand left her skin so he could shut off the water. He studied her back for a long minute before lifting his head until they stared at each other.

If Brenda could guess, she saw anguish in Rever's eyes reflecting what she was feeling. He definitely looked sad and she could relate, knowing Volder was going to take her away and there wasn't a damn thing either of them could do about it. Brenda knew Rever would keep her if he could but Rever was trapped with that bitch Tina as his bound, his hands tied by Zorn laws.

"Ral won't be able to stall Volder for long and Volder's job will make him return to his ship right away." Rever looked away from her but pain was definitely in his eyes. He took a shaky breath. "I have to let you go."

Without thinking, without caring if it was right or wrong, Brenda reached for the large man. Her hands opened on his shirt over his chest. Rever turned his head to stare down at her. She only hesitated for a second before running her hands up to cup his face, turning her body to face him, aware that she was naked but she didn't care.

Touching him was heaven and hell. Brenda had never been more drawn to a man in her life. Why couldn't they have met under other circumstances? If he wasn't bound already she'd beg him to keep her, to make her his.

Rever was such a wonderful man. If her husband on Earth had been a hundredth of the man that Rever was she never would have left him the first place. No matter what Tina did Rever never lost his temper and hurt her. It broke Brenda's heart that he was too damn good for the bitch he ended up with.

"Will you kiss me goodbye? I want the memory of what it's like to kiss you at least once to get me through the hell I'm facing. I can survive anything if I can just have that from you, Rever. Please? For just one damn minute let's forget we can't be together and say to hell with the law for just that tiny moment."

She was worried he'd say no, afraid he'd jerk away from her touching him when her hands caressed his jawline and her thumbs rubbed his cheeks, feeling how warm his skin was. He was so handsome to her in his wildly rugged way. His gaze was locked with hers as she got lost in the breathtaking depths of his eyes, seeing emotions flashing in the windows of his soul until he blinked, moving closer to her.

Relief hit her that he didn't distance himself but instead inched closer, his wide hips brushing her knees, and instantly Brenda spread them to allow him to get nearer to her. He stepped between her thighs, the material of his pants scratched a little on her tender skin but she barely noticed. He went chest to chest with her and two large arms wrapped around her waist while his face inched closer as he lowered his head. Their gazes remained locked until Brenda lowered her focus on his full lips that slightly parted, revealing sharp teeth that didn't frighten her. She opened her own mouth anticipating he was going to kiss her.

Shutting her eyes at the last second, she felt him hold her a little tighter a second before gentle lips brushed over hers, his breath warm on her skin. It stunned her that someone so damn strong could be so tender. His lips left hers as their breath mingled and then his lips returned.

Brenda opened her mouth to his fully when their tongues met. Her hands slid from his cheeks into his hair so she could pull him closer as his arms tightened around her body, drawing her into him. A sweet kiss quickly blazed out of control between them. He tasted so good to her, something sweet—similar to sugar—making her wonder why the guy always tasted candylike. Her curiosity dissipated when she felt the sharp tips of his teeth touch her lower lip but they didn't cut her as she explored his mouth. He groaned softly as the kiss intensified. Her ass left the counter when he lifted her higher up his body.

Wrapping her legs around his waist, she clung to him desperately, her body flaring to life under his mouth. The rough material of his pants brought awareness to her spread sex tightly pressed against him, making her ache with need for more than a kiss. Brenda moaned into his mouth, encouraging his arms to tighten around her even more until he held her so close that she could barely breathe but she didn't care. He was kissing her and he was holding her in his arms.

Rever tore his mouth away, breaking the kiss. A soft cry escaped her lips in protest. Brenda's eyes snapped open, just staring up at him, mere inches separating them, seeing torment in his blue eyes. They both were breathing hard.

"I want you so much it hurts," he said softly.

"Take me."

Pain flashed in his eyes. "We can't. Don't tempt me, Brenda."

"Do you love Tina?"

The pain in his eyes turned to rage in an instant. "No." The word was a snarl. "I can't stand her. It's you I want."

Pain flashed through her. "I hate this. I want to be with you and you want to be with me. I do not like your world right now with its damn rules."

Rever lowered his head to nuzzle her neck, hiding his face on her shoulder while his arms held her tightly, just standing in the middle of the bathroom with her naked and wrapped around him. He took deep breaths, his chest moving against hers.

Brenda clung to Rever knowing this was probably the last chance she'd ever get to memorize everything about him. He just held her as if she didn't weigh anything in his arms. Their gazes locked when he finally lifted his head and she saw something flicker in his eyes, an emotion she couldn't read but the tender look was gone. He slowly moved, walking the few steps to the sink.

It nearly broke her heart when Brenda felt Rever withdrawing from her both physically and emotionally. He eased her down until her ass touched the sink and then his hold on her loosened until he completely released her. Rever stepped back a foot and then another but his gaze remained locked on her. She was never going to see him again but she could at least take the memory of him and that kiss with her wherever she went. They were both trapped in what fate had handed them.

"There's only one thing to do."

"I know I have to go with him and you've made it clear that we have no choice."

His mouth tightened. "I don't want another male to claim you and you don't want Volder to touch your body. You should be mine."

Shock hit her at his words but then so did sadness. She totally agreed but they had no way to stop Volder from taking her. Rever's look hardened even more, a chilling coldness creeping into his eyes.

"I am a good warrior and an excellent fighter."

"You're going to challenge him?" Fear hit her. "You can't. You said you have no right to do that and it's against your laws. Won't you get arrested or something?"

He gave a jerk of a nod. "Yes. I would be punished severely and it is our way that I would be sent to a work camp for years."

She moved off the sink, her feet hitting the floor as she stood. "As much as I want to be with you that won't work. You'd be sent away, we still couldn't be together and I won't let you do that for me, to sacrifice yourself that way."

Rever hesitated. "I will return in a minute after I get your clothing." He slowly looked down her body, a soft growl rumbling from his throat. "I want you too much to look at you like this. You are going to make me break my control again and I can't do that right now."

Brenda watched Rever spin on his heel to storm out of the bathroom. She turned, gripping the sink, and lowered her head in defeat. She was going to have no choice but to go with Volder. She sighed.

"It's time to put on the big girl panties and just suck it up," she ordered herself in a whisper.

In less than a minute Rever returned, dropping her bag on the bathroom floor. She turned her head to meet his gorgeous eyes. The cold look was still there telling her silently that he'd hardened his heart against her. She almost felt grateful that he was such a strong man, reminding her that she needed to be strong as well.

Wailing and throwing herself at his feet to beg him to keep her wasn't going to do any good except it might get him killed or sent away to a Zorn work camp, which was probably comparable to prison. She cared about him too damn much to be that selfish by begging him to do something stupid on her behalf that wouldn't even change the outcome. Rever would be locked up and she'd be forced to be with another man. She straightened her shoulders, meeting his gaze.

"Get dressed and put on pants. It will be cold where you are going."

She nodded, looking away from him. Rever spun away, storming back out of the bathroom. Forcing her body to move, she bent over, removing her clothes from her bag. Her back ached a little where she was scratched but it was just a small discomfort while she dressed. Ali had supplied her with new socks and boots so she put those on last.

In minutes Rever was back, pausing at the doorway. She frowned as she studied him, noticing that he'd changed clothes, and she couldn't help but stare at his black uniform. He looked dangerously sexy in the thick leather that molded to his body. He had weapons strapped to his hips and more strapped to his powerfully built thighs and she studied the mean looking knife handles sticking out of sheathes that were strapped to him. Her gaze lifted to meet his.

"Let's go. We don't have much time." He held out his hand to her, his blue eyes glowed with intensity.

"Go where?" Her gaze flew to his outfit again, thinking he looked ready for battle. Her heart nearly stopped at that thought and her gaze flew back to his.

He took a deep breath. "I spent years patrolling the Outlander area. If anyone can survive with a woman out there it is me. As I said, I'm a damn good fighter, Brenda. It will be dangerous and it could get us both killed but we can be together." He paused, his gaze locked with hers. "It is your choice. We'll be hunted but I'm a warrior who will be on a familiar battlefield. It is the only chance we have to find happiness with each other."

Everything he'd said about working in the Outlander area slammed into her, about how women didn't live out there because it was too brutal a place with criminals and wild Zorn males. Fear hit her but as she stared up at Rever, something else hit her too, the realization that she'd rather die with Rever than live without him was crystal clear to her. She swallowed as she took a step forward, reaching for his hand, nodding.

"I'd follow you to hell and back, Rever. I just want to be with you."

Rever smiled as his large warm hand clasped her smaller one. "Get your bag. You'll need clothing."

Blinking away relieved tears that he was willing to risk everything for her, she bent, gripping her belongings. She looked up at him. "Thank you."

His smile died. "Don't thank me for the very selfish thing I do. I will probably get both of us killed just for my desire to keep you with me. I don't know how long Ral will keep Volder away but when they realize we have run together the hunt will begin so we need to go quickly now."

A shiver of dread hit her. "They really will hunt us? Seriously?"

He gave a grim nod. "It is the Zorn way."

"Then let's get the hell out of here."

Rever suddenly moved, bending just enough that his lips brushed her forehead. He nodded as he stepped back.

"We must hurry. I want to reach the Outlander area before night falls and we have a stop to make first."

Chapter Seven

ഇ

"Don't speak," Rever said softly half an hour later.

Brenda studied the building they stopped in front of in the middle of the woods but in the distance she saw a large wall. The top of it was thick like a catwalk and it had big, black-outfitted Zorn men who were carrying weapons that resembled guns as they walked along the length of it. If she didn't miss her guess, this had to be some kind of border crossing. She gave a nod that she understood his command.

Rever's face went blank of emotion as he took a deep breath. He released her hand, his gaze roaming the area, and looked to be waiting for something. It didn't take long before two large men in the same outfit that Rever wore walked out of the dense trees next to the building. They looked mean and carried as many weapons strapped on their bodies as he did.

"Argis Rever." One of them nodded. "Is this an inspection?"

"My father has instructed me to give this human woman a tour. She is an ambassador from Earth and she wants shown how we protect our cities."

The other man frowned. "Why here? It is too dangerous."

"I am not taking her past the zone line." Rever shot the guard a dirty look. "She was curious about the Outlander areas so I am giving her a tour of the supply building to show her how prepared we are and that other human women would be safe in our cities. If she sees how we protect our citizens she will recommend to her Earth that they send more human females." Rever smiled. "Wouldn't it be nice to have thousands of them available to bound with?"

Both men turned their full attention on Brenda. She lifted her chin, putting on her best game face, and tried to not to curl her lip as both men leered at her, openly staring at about every inch of her body. One of them grinned.

"She has that much power over her women?"

Nodding sharply, Rever lied. "She is very important on her world. Upon her recommendation a lot more human women will travel to Zorn to bound with our males. My father is a great leader who always wants to please his people."

The dark-eyed man grinned. "Is this one bound?"

Rever tensed. "She is an ambassador. Control yourself. She is just here for a tour. Let's go. She has a banquet to attend in an hour. Take us inside now."

Both guards turned, striding for the building. Brenda darted a glance at Rever. He met her look with a nod, motioning her forward. Her backpack was hidden in the woods so she didn't have the weight to slow her down as she almost ran after the much taller men who had damn long legs. They rounded the building and she saw two thick steel-looking doors that both of the guards paused in front of. The door slid wide open after one of them slapped his palm to a control pad.

"I am Borvon." The tall blond man smiled at Brenda, his attention darting to her breasts and then back to her face. "We are heavily supplied in case of attack. Our males are the best warriors handpicked by Rever for our fighting skills. We have never had a breach. Your women would be very safe in our cities."

Giving a nod, Brenda attempted to look impressed. She'd never taken acting classes but for some reason Rever wanted her to pretend to be someone really important. She had no idea how they'd get past those guards on the wall with their weapons but she trusted that Rever knew what he was doing even if she didn't. Since he wanted her to play a part, she'd try her best to pull it off.

"Argis Rever," she said softly. "I see you do handpick the best warriors. They look very capable."

Full lips curved upward as Rever's gaze met hers, seeing amusement flash there for just a heartbeat before it was gone.

"Of course. I told you that your human women would be secure living in our cities with our men patrolling the borders. We keep the wilder, less civilized Zorn on the other side of the walls. We are slowly controlling more of the Outlander areas until eventually there will be order all over Zorn. It is just a slow process since some resist change."

"I see." She gave a nod.

When they were led inside the supply building, Brenda saw motorcycle-type vehicles parked near the doors. Weapons were stacked on shelves along one wall and there were uniforms hanging neatly from hooks. The room was filled with a large assortment of other gear and sealed boxes. She eyed it trying to pretend as if she were greatly impressed. Rever moved, getting behind both men. She turned her attention on the guards, smiling at them and watched as both men leered openly at her body again.

Rever moved quickly, gripping both males to slam their heads together hard. Brenda was shocked at the sudden violence. The guards went down to the floor with Rever's help as he carefully lowered them so they didn't slam into the hard surface. He sighed, releasing both limp men before straightening. Their gaze met.

"They will be fine. I hated to do that but I knew they wouldn't leave us alone in here to take what we need. I trained them too well than to make that mistake. Get out of your clothes."

Her mouth fell open. "What?"

"Strip now. Take it all off."

"Strip?" She darted a look at the two men on the floor, then looked up at Rever's amused expression. "Why?"

"I'm putting you in a uniform. It will be large but we have smaller sizes available for training our younger males. If we dress right they will think we are going on patrol and if we wear helmets on the vehicle they can't see our faces when we drive right past the guards. They won't stay unconscious long so hurry, Brenda. We need to get beyond the wall before they wake up to raise the alarm."

She reached for her shirt as Rever spun away, walking for the uniforms. She carefully watched the men on the floor, praying they didn't wake while she was naked and thought that would be awkward if they did. Stripping quickly, she turned around and nearly bumped into Rever.

He was staring at every exposed inch of her naked body. He softly growled when he thrust out a uniform to her. "Dress quickly. I couldn't find footings that would fit you so wear your boots."

Brenda stared up into his eyes, spotting lust burning in their blue depths as his focus lingered on her breasts. Tearing her gaze from his, she glanced at the two down men who were still unconscious. She shifted her attention to the front of Rever's tight pants, seeing the hard, undeniable bulge that was evident. He looked uncomfortable trapped in leather that way. The man was built and those things were too tight. As she watched, his hips shifted and she saw the movement for what it really was. He was trying to adjust to a more comfortable stance. Her chin rose as she looked upward.

His blue eyes were incredible, making her decide he was the sexist man alive, either alien or human, and her body instantly responded to the need reflected in his gaze. She licked her lips and took a step toward him, wanting him as much as he wanted her.

A soft growl came from him. "Brenda..."

"You can't walk that way." She darted a glance at the front of his pants. "You'll hurt yourself trying."

"We don't have time for this."

Her focus lifted to stare at his face. "I want you so badly that just the thought of you inside me makes me want to come. Do you know what a quickie is? We're both on edge. I bet you could make me come really fast and judging by how hard you are, you won't last long either. What are a few minutes anyway? Think about how good it would feel. I've wanted you so much it hurts ever since the alley."

A snarl left his lips as he dropped the uniform on the floor. He spun away, moving fast for the corner. "You tempt me but it wouldn't be safe for me to take you with those males on the floor, Brenda. They could wake up and I would be distracted so they could easily overpower me. I'll handle you in a minute."

Disappointment struck hard. She thought he'd take her up on her offer but instead Rever was moving away. She watched him grab something from the wall before he spun back around. She heard a clank noise and saw the restraints in his hands.

"Kinky. Are you going to punish me for trying to tempt you into doing something dangerous like fucking me while we're here?" She grinned as she teased him.

He paused walking, his head tilted. "Kinky? I don't understand the word."

"Are those for me?" She turned slowly, presenting him with her back. Brenda spread her thighs apart a little and bent forward, moving her hands to her ass to clasp them together there. "You could put those on me and fuck me. That would be kinky."

Rever growled again, shaking his head as he advanced. He walked around her to crouch down by the two men. She straightened up knowing playtime was over and watched Rever yank their hands behind their backs. Instead of hooking them up one at a time, he turned both guards so they were back to back, chaining them together by crossing the restraints so a left wrist was hooked to the right wrist of the other man and vice-versa. With them facing away from each other, chained together, it would make even getting up off the floor a very difficult joint venture. Rever rose to his feet.

He turned to face Brenda. "Now you."

Brenda glanced at his empty hands when he moved forward in a few long strides. She gasped as he gripped her hips, lifting her from the floor until she was pressed firmly against his leather-covered chest. Rever took another step until she was pinned between him and a cold support beam that he gently leaned them both against. Big hands slid to her ass so he could position her higher up his tall frame.

Their gazes locked together, his free hand went between them to tear open the front of his pants. Brenda's heart pounded while she stared into his beautiful eyes, which narrowed. His long, black eyelashes closed for a second in relief when he freed his cock from the tight constraint of his pants. His eyes opened, meeting hers again.

"I will try to be gentle but I want you badly."

Her arms wrapped around his neck as she wrapped her legs around his hips. She felt the rough material of his pants with the back of her legs and against her inner thighs where she gripped him. She nodded.

"I'm so wet and ready for you."

A soft growl tore from Rever a heartbeat before his mouth was suddenly over hers, forcefully demanding entrance. Full lips pressed hers apart easily as she opened up to him as his tongue swept into her mouth. Rever's hips shifted slightly a second before the head of his thick cock pressed against her pussy. He growled, his tongue stilling when he pushed upward.

A moan tore from Brenda, which he captured with his mouth as he entered her slowly. Her body stretched to accommodate him. His hand that had freed him from his pants wrapped around her waist so he could hold her tightly as he sank deeper into her. When he was fully inside her body he held still for long seconds.

It was heaven and hell having Rever inside her, it felt that incredible and that wonderful feeling was the heaven part. The hellish part was he stayed still, buried in her until she bucked her hips, silently pleading with him to move. Her body ached for him almost painfully. When she said she was wet and ready for him she hadn't been kidding.

Rever tore his mouth completely from hers so they could look at each other. He swiped his bottom lip with his tongue, breathing faster than normal, and didn't say a word. He just moved, withdrawing almost out of her completely a second before he thrust upward. It was a fast motion that made Brenda cry out. Rever froze.

"Am I hurting you? You're so tight."

She realized her eyes were closed. She opened them to meet his intense gaze again. "No. That was pleasure. God, Rever. Move. Please."

He growled. She didn't have to tell him twice. He shifted his hold on her so he held her ass in both of his hands, holding her up, his body pinning her between his wide chest and the cold, hard support beam behind her more firmly. He moved then, fucking her in hard drives.

Brenda gripped the top of his shoulders, her legs locked tighter around his waist as he pounded fast and deep. The sensations were slamming her as hard as his cock was. It was pleasure and almost pain at the same time to have something as thick as Rever moving inside her. He hit nerves she never knew she had before. She put her head back, leaning it against the support, eyes shut, as moans tore from her.

Rever shifted his hips a little so every motion rubbed against her clit. That was all it took for the pleasure to explode into overdrive. She felt her inner vaginal muscles tightening, tensing for release. Rever groaned loudly, his face falling forward to bury against her shoulder and neck. He pumped frantically into her, a new level of ecstasy making Brenda claw at his leather-clad shoulders, knowing her nails were biting into the thick material while she moaned his name, nearly chanting it.

Brenda gasped and then threw her own face forward. She opened her mouth against his shirt, screaming out her climax as it gripped her brutally, spreading through her, and pleasure felt as if it were tearing her apart. Rever jerked hard, his thrusts tightening in small motions, a snarl tearing from his lips into her skin as he followed her, coming hard deep inside her body. They held onto each other tightly as their bodies rode the after-passion effects of great sex until Rever stilled completely.

They were two sexual heartbeats together. His cock throbbed as her inner pussy walls twitched from the aftermath of their hot quickie. The only sound in the room was their heavy breathing. Rever's arms loosened slightly so his hold on her ass wasn't bruising, and she was certain there would be bruises but she didn't give a damn if his entire handprints were in black and blue where he'd gripped her while fucking her. She'd wear them proudly.

A smile curved her lips at the contemplation that she was feeling as if she'd been fucked within an inch of her life. She'd always wondered about that saying and now that she knew, experiencing it firsthand was pretty damn amazing. Her arms wrapped tighter around his shoulders as she inhaled his scent, loving being held in his arms and enjoying him being inside her. The fact that he'd just made her come harder than she had in her life wasn't lost on her either.

Rever turned his face, nuzzling her tender skin under her ear at the line of her throat. "You're mine," he rasped against her skin. "I claim you, Brenda. I bound to you. You are of my heart and you are worth everything to me. We'll survive together. There is nothing but us together. From this day forward, I vow a new life with you as my bound."

His words stunned her but made her heart swell. She turned her head, putting enough space between them to see his face. When he lifted his head their gazes locked and Brenda had to blink back tears. She released her hold around his neck to cup his face, thinking that he was incredibly handsome. She saw tenderness and what resembled love in his eyes as they stared at each other.

"I love you, Rever. You've made me the happiest woman and I promise you that I'll do everything to make you happy too. I think I have an idea what you've given up to be with me and I can't believe you'd walk away from your life like you did but I'm so damn grateful we're together. I'll make it up to you somehow by being the best damn bound ever."

His lips curved upward as he grinned, reaching up to hold her with one arm while he caressed her cheek. His fingers brushed down the line of her jaw to her chin, tipping her head up so their lips were inches apart.

"I know we will be happy together and I know I made the right choice. I only hope that I can keep you safe." His smile died. "Our only chance of being able to stay together is if we go to the Outland area but it will be very dangerous. I thought about trying to get us off world but they will be looking for us at every checkpoint once they realize I've taken you. You belong to Volder according to our law and if we're captured they will return you to him." He paused, an intensity burned in the blue depths of his eyes. "You're my bound, Brenda."

She nodded. "I'm yours, Rever. I belong to you."

He softly growled. "We need to go." A small smile teased his lips. "Put clothes on. You always tempt me and make me lose my control. I wanted to wait until we were safe to share this with you."

She smiled back. "I'm glad this happened right here and right now. I ached for you and you have no idea how much I've wanted this."

"I do know since I've wanted you as much as you wanted me. It has been torture resisting the urge to take you as often as I have wished I could." He gently put her down on the floor. "Get dressed. They will wake soon and we need to be across the border before they do."

She dressed quickly, watching Rever grab empty bags, filling them with supplies around the room and strapping all four bags on the motorcycle-looking vehicle closest to the door. Her heart was pounding with fear and excitement over having to get across the border without detection. The uniform was leather, the shirt and the pants were a little big on her, but she hoped from a distance that she could fool the guards into thinking she was a young man. Rever finished supplying the two-wheeled vehicle and then crouched down by the men to check on them. His head rose.

"Stay while I retrieve your backpack from the woods. Don't move. If one of them wakes I want you to hit him." He stood up, walking to a wall, and jerked down what resembled a baton from a shelf. He turned, striding for her. "Here. Hit the back of the head but not too hard. I don't want them to die."

"I don't either."

He gave a jerk of his head before he was gone. She guarded the two men on the floor feeling dread at the notion of them waking up, not wanting to hit either man. She sat down to put on her boots to finish getting ready while she waited and watched the guards. In minutes relief hit her when Rever returned with her backpack. He held it while she stood up and then handed it over to her.

"They will open the gate when they see us approach and you wearing this will help hide your smaller frame from the guard's notice if you put it on. Hang onto me tightly, Brenda. If things go bad we will flee and the territory out there is very harsh so the ride may grow difficult."

He got on the big bike. She hesitated and then climbed on the wide seat behind him. Rever handed her a big helmet. She figured out the strap easily enough since it was similar to the ones at home, only the face shielding was tinted a dark blue. Her arms wrapped around Rever as he started the motor. She noticed then that he'd opened both double doors when he'd returned with her backpack.

"Don't speak if they stop us."

"I could have guessed that since you said I'm supposed to be a boy."

A chuckle sounded from Rever. "Are you ready, Brenda? Are you sure you want to do this?" He turned his head.

She couldn't see his face with the tinted helmet on, making his features nothing but a shadow. That meant he couldn't see her face either, which was a good thing, she decided, because she was terrified. She hoped he couldn't smell that. Everything he'd said about the Outlander area told her it was as dangerous as hell.

"I'm sure. I want to be with you and if this is the only way then let's go."

He turned back around, lifting his boot, and the vehicle slowly pulled forward. She was surprised at how quietly the motor ran. She felt the vibration of it but there really wasn't much of a sound except a soft hum. Rever drove them out of the building to a dirt road leading toward the wall. As they drew closer Brenda couldn't see around Rever's tall frame and wide back so she clung tighter to his waist.

Rever lifted an arm, motioning to someone. Brenda shut her eyes, just praying they weren't going to be caught. When the bike slowed but didn't stop, she opened her eyes just in time to see a guard was standing there holding open the gate as they rode past. She stared at the Zorn guard but he didn't look at them. He was holding the gate in one hand, a weapon in the other, while he scanned the area they were heading for.

Were attacks that bad that the man was constantly on alert like that? That thought sent a shiver of fear through Brenda. She was about to experience the Outlander area herself. *Can Rever really keep me safe?* She hoped so when she gripped him tighter as their speed increased as he gave the machine more power.

A few minutes later his body relaxed. "We're clear." He spoke just loud enough for her to hear him. "We're out of range of them stopping us and the patrols are shallow this far out. Now we just have to worry about the residents. We're heading into the remote and harsh mountains to the third moon region. It's difficult to reach it without a vehicle so many of the wild males won't go there but I've been there plenty of times. I think it is the safest and best location for us to live."

"I trust you." She meant it.

Rever kept them at a fast pace even after the sun went down. Brenda was glad she couldn't see what they were driving on because judging by the way her ass hurt from slamming and jarring on the seat, the terrain had to be pretty rough. Hours seemed to pass before the bike finally slowed.

Rever shut it off, turned his head, and looked back at her. It was dark except for the headlights still on so she could make him out since the lights were behind him. She eased her hold on him as he gave her a nod, climbing off, and stretched his arms and legs. She was stiff herself after the hours of holding onto him tightly on the rough ride.

"We'll have to walk the rest of the way but we are close."

She climbed off the seat and did a little stretching of her own. Her ass felt numb but sensation returned in a few minutes while she stared up at the three moons, all placed in different areas of the night sky. Bright stars shone in the clear night. The smell of the woods on Zorn was very similar to Earth with the strong tree and dirt scents. She could see the shapes of tall trees around them, nothing more than dark shadows in the night.

"Where are we? What is around us?"

"There is a cave up ahead with water that we'll move into. We will survive nicely there and it will be comfortable. I will take good care of you, Brenda."

"I know you will."

He turned and she saw him doing something to the bike. In seconds she realized he was unloading it. She moved closer.

"Let me help."

"Your vision isn't as good as mine. I'm going to leave you here and pack these in but I won't be long." He reached up, removed his helmet, and took a deep breath of fresh air as he set it on the seat. "I don't scent anyone nearby and I would with the wind blowing. I know the patrols hit just weeks ago clearing this entire area out so no one will return for a long time. Very few of the wild ones venture this way and when they do I will easily run them off."

"I'd rather go with you. I don't want to be alone."

Two large hands gripped her hips as he turned to face her. "I will move faster without you and I won't be long. I wouldn't leave you if I thought you were in danger. The supplies are heavy and I have to make a few trips. We have wild animals in the Outlander areas so I want to make sure none of them have taken up the cave before I take you there."

Brenda swallowed. "What kind of animals? Will they attack me while you're gone?"

Rever chuckled. "No. They don't like lights while they hunt at night so I left them on. You will be safe if you stay by the light. If you hear anything approaching move in front in the vehicle and they won't come near you."

The warning frightened her more than just a little. *What did Zorn wildlife look like?* If one of those scary looking *killis* had been harmless she really didn't want to see something that wasn't. *How dangerous were the local animal residents?* She nodded though, knowing she'd be brave if it killed her. Rever had gone on the run with her, leaving his life, his home and his job behind to keep her. The least she could do was woman up and not be a wimp. She straightened her shoulders and forced a smile since he said he had good night vision.

"I'll be fine. Don't worry about me."

Rever chuckled again. "You are quite a human."

109

If he only knew, she thought silently, keeping her smile in place. He released her, turned back to the bike and untied two of the large supply bags. He gave her one last look and then walked away into the darkness. Brenda waited until she couldn't hear his soft tread before she almost ran into the headlights to stand in the beams, eyeing the darkness around her with fear.

She sat down after a while in red dirt. Brenda startled, her heart pounding, when a while later a growl sounded from somewhere not too far off. She hoped that was Rever but she inched to the center of the lights though just in case it wasn't. Minutes later she heard him approach, his boots crunching on the hard packed dirt, and saw his large figure looming, getting closer.

"I told you it wouldn't take long."

She climbed to her feet, brushing off her ass. "Do I get to go with you this time?"

"Yes. I can carry the last two bags if you can follow with your backpack. Can you walk in the darkness? If you can't see I'll make a third trip to carry you on my shoulder."

"I'll make it. I heard a growl."

"It was an *obrion*."

"A what?"

Rever chuckled. "They look similar to a *killis* that is not small, not round, and it does eat meat. They are dangerous but I am with you."

"So it won't attack?" She was hopeful.

He hesitated. "It won't attack twice if it dares a first attempt. I will protect you."

She nodded, knowing Rever was one large warrior and was pretty sure he could take care of whatever lurked out there. She watched him untie the remaining two bags and then kill the light from the vehicle, making darkness surround them. She blinked a few times feeling relief as her eyes adjusted to it. She couldn't see really well but the three moons were bright enough in the clear sky that she could see outlines.

"Let's go."

She nodded, following the large moving shape in front of her, and made sure she stayed close. Rever could quickly cover some serious ground with his longer legs but instead he moved slowly just so she could keep up easier. They traveled about half a mile uphill before she saw a large, darker shape ahead that resembled a black hole to her. When Rever kept moving for it she assumed that was the cave entrance.

Rever stopped outside of it. "Don't move until I return after I light a fire. I was in too much of a hurry to bring you here to take the time before."

She was surprised that he came back so quickly within a few minutes. He didn't say a word but just walked up to her, bent and then lifted her into his strong arms. She gasped out a second before she wrapped her arms around his neck. She had to be pretty heavy with her added backpack but he didn't seem to notice or care. He walked into the dark opening and then turned. Light flickered ahead.

The cave he walked into was larger than she expected and she couldn't help but stare at the twenty-by-thirty-foot room. As she studied the back wall she realized that water was running down it to disappear along the lower portion of the floor she couldn't see in the shadows. Her gaze turned on the circular rock structure in the center of the cave that was burning, softly lighting up the room.

"You had time to build a fire pit?"

"I told you it was rare that some of the Outlander males came out this far but some have. They have built in many conveniences inside this cave when they were living here. They left plenty of wood for burning when the patrols cleared them out weeks ago so we are better off than I thought we would be." He gently put her down on her feet.

She stared openly at the cave as she removed her backpack, dropping it to the ground, and her eyes returned to the back wall where water flowed down it to disappear into the floor. She moved forward and realized there was a large gap between the back of the cave and the hard-packed dirt. She moved even closer to stare down at a four-foot-wide pool.

"The water is not too deep and is safe to bathe in."

She turned around to find Rever watching her with tense, rugged features. She tilted her head, staring at him, wondering what he was thinking.

He hesitated. "I must hide the rover vehicle so they won't spot it if they patrol this area again. I don't expect them to but I would rather do it in case they do circle back. I don't want us found." He walked forward, staring down at her. "I want you to bathe while I am gone."

"Okay." She gave him a nod. "I probably do have a coat of dirt on me." She looked down at the leather, seeing how dusty it was from the rough ride on the motorcycle-like vehicle. Her gaze lifted to his. "Should I wait for you?" A smile teased her lips. "I could wash your back."

A soft growl rumbled from him. "I want to do that with you but later. It's our bounding night. I want you to bathe and be naked when I return. Can you set up our bed?"

Her heart missed a beat as she nodded. "It's like our honeymoon, isn't it?"

His mouth curved downward. "I don't know that term."

"A bounding night means we're going to have a lot of sex, doesn't it?"

A grin bloomed. "Yes."

"I'll get the bath and put a bed down while you go hide the bike, but hurry." She grinned at him.

He pointed to a bag. "Use three mats located there to make us a bed in the corner." He pointed to a flat spot on the floor. His head turned so their gazes locked again. "I will be fast and I would like you on the mats naked when I return.

Will you do this for me? I know human women don't like to be told what to do but I would appreciate it if you could to this for me."

Moving closer to him, Brenda reached up to put her hand on his chest. "I'll be bathed, naked and spread out on that bed waiting for you. I'm not her, I'm nothing like her." Brenda didn't even want to say Tina's name.

Rever nodded. "I know this. I'll be back."

Chapter Eight

ଛ

The mats were laid out in the corner. Stacked together they were comfortable, inches of soft padding between the hard, unforgiving cave floor and her body. Brenda was naked, clean and shivering just a little. The fire helped heat the room but Rever would warm her up a hell of a lot better.

She'd hurried to get ready but wondered what was taking him so long. Rever had been gone for almost an hour at her guess and she couldn't wait for him to return. She was sitting on the bedding with her attention fixed on the opening curve of the cave.

Movement finally caught her eye as Rever walked inside and shock hit her, seeing him wet and totally naked except for his boots that he toed off just inside the room, kicking them out of the way. She stared open-mouthed as he slowly stalked toward her, thinking he was absolutely beautiful and incredibly sexy. Muscles rippled along his body as he closed the distance between them and Brenda had to remember to breathe.

Rever stopped feet in front of her while she stared up his body, noticing that he was aroused in all his glory. She couldn't help but focus her attention on his erect cock. The guy was thick, hard, and just as sexy as could be. He moved again, dropping to his knees, which drew her attention to his broad chest where wetness glistened on his skin making it appear that he'd been oiled to add to his beauty. She watched a few drops of water slide down his chest, one hovering at his puckered nipple.

Brenda finally remembered she could move, leaning forward slowly she got to her hands and knees to inch forward, crawling the few remaining feet between them. A soft growl rumbled from Rever's slightly parted lips. His cock jerked slightly as she drew so close she was a breath away from him. She rose up on her knees so they faced each other, moving inches closer to him. Her sole focus fixed on that drop of water on his nipple that she didn't hesitate to go for with her mouth.

Her tongue darted out to catch the drip before it fell. Rever tensed, his stomach muscles tightening so that every distinctive ridge lightly quivered. Her mouth closed over his nipple as her tongue swirled in a circular pattern over the bud. She tugged him into her mouth, sucking on him.

Two large, hot hands wrapped around her to cup her ass firmly, his fingers gripping her curved flesh. His chest vibrated against her nose and chin when another growl rumbled from Rever. His cock pressed into her soft belly when his hands yanked her closer until she found herself flattened against his large, firm body in a heartbeat. The hands squeezed her ass tightly, drawing a moan from her.

"Brenda," his voice was husky, deep. "Release me."

With regret she let go of him with a soft *pop* sound. She lifted her chin so she could appreciate the sight of his chest, taking in every inch of him as she slowly looked up to his chin to see that his head was tilted down. His incredible blue eyes were glowing when their gazes locked together. The hands gripping her lifted, her knees left the soft mat as he drew her body higher on his, never looking away from each other until they were nose to nose, literally touching.

"You are mine."

She didn't hesitate. "I am."

His big body shivered a little but she knew he wasn't cold. He took a deep breath, smashing her breasts even tighter against his chest. His hard cock was digging into her thigh now but it wasn't uncomfortable. His hands eased their hold slowly, lowering her down again until her knees were touching the mat.

"Present yourself to me."

Brenda swallowed hard, letting go of him as his hands left her ass. She walked backward on her knees to put a little space between them and then hesitated.

"Do you want me on my back with my legs spread or do you want me this way?"

She turned around, dropping her hands to the mat so she was on her hands and knees. She turned her head, watching his face over her shoulder while she spread her thighs apart, bracing her knees. She knew what kind of picture she made as she spread her legs a little more and bent her arms enough to push her ass higher.

Rever admired the view, softly snarling a second before he inched behind her to curve his hands around her bent body. His full attention remained on her ass as his big hands slid along the curve from her thighs to her lower back, then down again. One hand slid between her legs, brushing against her pussy.

Brenda closed her eyes as Rever's fingers explored her already wet sex, two of them teasing her slit, testing her, and pressed against her entrance but didn't enter her. His digits slid lower and rubbed against her clit. He separated her with his fingers a little wider, just enough for her swelling bud to slide between those fingers before he pinched the sensitive flesh gently, trapping it to rub back and forth between his knuckles. A moan broke from Brenda's lips.

"That feels so good."

Rever's response was another growl. There was something so primitive and male when he made those deep, rumbling sounds that turned her on more. He was such a big, powerful man, strong, huge really. But his touch was gentle as he continued to capture Brenda's clit between his fingers, pushing them tighter against the curve of her body, which caused her sensitized nub to push out farther from between both digits. His thumb suddenly pushed inside her pussy, breaching her.

A louder moan tore from Brenda at the wonderful sensation of having him inside her. She dropped her elbows to the mat to tilt her body more to give him freer access to her. She closed her eyes, lowering her face so her forehead touched the soft mat. She wiggled her ass as his thumb pushed in deeper.

"Please."

"Silence," he ordered. "Feel."

She was feeling the urge to scream in frustration a minute later, something she fought to stifle when his thumb eased out of her. His fingers tugged at her clit one last time before he released it, removing his hand entirely from her. Shocked that he'd stopped, Brenda groaned in frustration then. She lifted up and turned her head to stare at him over her shoulder, watching him move back a few inches.

She was shocked as Rever rolled over. She tensed her arms, pushing her upper body up, wondering what in the hell he was doing. He was on his back with his face between where her calves were but then he inched upward, wiggling between her spread legs. She gasped in shock as he gripped her hips, lifting her body up, pulling her back a foot until her knees were just above his shoulders. He jerked her hips closer to his face so his mouth could captured her clit and his hands shifted their hold so he could spread her folds wider apart.

Shock turned into moans of pleasure, Rever holding her in place as his mouth tormented her clit. Brenda had never been in the position before of being over a man's face, almost sitting on him. It was what she was doing only she was careful to not put weight down. The sensation was raw and wonderful as Rever's mouth sucked and teased, Brenda moaned louder and writhed in pleasure. Throwing her head back, she cried out as she came hard when his teeth scrapped against her swollen bud. Ecstasy hammered her.

Rever let go of her clit and Brenda could only gasp as he breached her pussy with his thick tongue, it feeling big as he pushed inside her. He growled loudly, slowly fucking her with it while her muscles twitched in the aftermath of release. Withdrawing from her slowly, she heard a snarl came from him as he lifted her enough for him to wiggle out from beneath her.

Brenda collapsed on her elbows and knees, feeling shaky. Rever's large body dropped around hers suddenly as he caged her in his arms on his hands and knees over her. The only warning she got was a nudge against her pussy from the thick head of his cock before he pushed into her slowly, not stopping until he was seated fully inside.

"Oh God," she gasped. "You're so damn big."

"You're so tight," he groaned. "Lord of the Moons, woman. You are perfect."

He started to move in slow thrusts that left Brenda without the ability to think, only able to just feel. Rever was amazingly gentle until he increased the pace slightly. His hands left the floor as he straightened behind her, gripping her hips to hold her steady while he moved faster and harder inside her, creating a different sensation.

Brenda clawed at the mat under her, using it to brace her body as moans tore from her throat. With every stroke Rever felt good but when he pulled almost completely out of her, then slammed back in, it felt even better. He twisted his hips a little in a move that had his balls tapping against her clit with every motion as he positioned her a little with his hands to spread her thighs wider.

Raw bliss coursed through her feeling his rock-hard, thick cock rubbing against her tightly, creating havoc on her inner nerves. With the added stimulation against her clit it was sensory overload causing her muscles to tighten with anticipation of the coming climax, a warning that she wasn't going to last much longer.

"I'm going to…" she gasped.

"Come for me," Rever groaned. "Now."

Four more hard thrusts from his hips and she did. Brenda nearly screamed as her vaginal muscles quivered hard. She went into spasms as rapture tore through her body, a blinding explosion of ecstasy seizing her. Behind her Rever roared out his release as he came and she could feel it deep inside her pussy, filling her with his semen in hard bursts of spreading warmth.

She would have collapsed in the aftermath if Rever wasn't firmly gripping her hips. She panted, sweat tickling her and her eyes were closed. Rever bent over her again, his hand releasing one of her hips to brace that hand on the mat next her shoulder. His long hair fell around them in a dark curtain as his large body molded against her back. She opened her eyes to stare at the stark contrast of his black long locks mixing with her blonde hair. Rever nuzzled her head with his.

"You are mine and I am yours. We are bound."

A smile curved her lips. He was going to keep saying it, it seemed, and she wasn't ever going to get tired of hearing it.

"Yes."

"You make me happy, Brenda."

"You make me happy too, Rever."

He moved, slowly withdrawing from her body to stretch out next to her, pulling her down on the mat with him. She ended up lying half on his massive chest, half on the mat as he sprawled on his back. His fingers ran through her hair, his other hand lightly brushing her back as he held her.

"Life will be harsh but I will do my best to make it easy for you."

Lifting her head, she stared into his beautiful eyes. "I don't need easy. I just need you."

His sharper teeth peeked from his full lips as he smiled. "You are very special."

"So are you."

They smiled at each other. Brenda was still amazed that he'd left his life behind to be with her and she was grateful too. Her smile slowly died. She moved, lifting up enough to inch higher on his body to stare down at him.

"What made you decide to bring me out here?"

His smile died. "I couldn't stand the thought of Volder taking you from me and I couldn't let you go. I resisted how I was drawn to you, what I felt, but seeing him there made me realize it was going to truly happen. He terrified you and he abused you." His tone grew harsh. "You should be cherished and the idea of him allowing other men to force you to your knees to tongue them sent rage through me. I knew then that I couldn't allow it to happen." He paused. "And kissing you was my breaking point. I just couldn't let you go."

She stared into his eyes thinking, *it isn't a confession of undying love but I'll take it*. She nodded. "I'm glad you did. I'd rather live in a cave with you than be anywhere else, with anyone else."

"Life will be harsh for us, more for you than for me because I was raised to be a warrior. We live in tough conditions with our training but you are human. I will care for you, Brenda. I will protect you and make sure you never go hungry."

Reaching up, she caressed his cheek. "I know. You don't have to convince me."

He smiled. "I am a good hunter and provider."

Laughing, she nodded. "I believe that."

His smile died. "I worry about the future."

"As long as I'm with you it's all right."

"They will hunt for us but I will kill anyone who comes to try to take you away from me and I will kill any wild males who sniff around our home. I am concerned about when I get you with offspring since you are human and not as rugged as a Zorn woman. If you need medical help I worry about getting you there safely in time and what will happen if we have to go back."

She swallowed hard, not wanting to think about a possible pregnancy living in a cave. "What will happen if we ever have to go back?"

Rever's eyes narrowed, a soft growl came from him as anger tightened his features. "Volder will try to take you from me since the law will be on his side and I can't challenge him since according to our laws I am still bound to Tina. He has a right to you so I will be locked up for your theft. I don't worry about myself but I worry about you. Volder will punish you for running away with me. Swear that if you're ever captured you will lie by telling him that I took you by force."

Shock hit her. "I will never say that. You saved me."

Brenda could only gasp as her back hit the mat when he rolled them over quickly, coming down on top of her to pin her under his massive body in the blink of an eye. He growled softly while his gaze narrowed and he stared into her eyes.

"You don't understand. Abusing a woman is forbidden but there are circumstances on Zorn where punishing a woman is acceptable and running away with a male is one of those offenses. You will tell them I took you by force, holding you against your will if we are ever taken back, Brenda. You don't understand what he could do to you."

She wasn't afraid of Rever as she reached up to cup his face, even though he looked seriously pissed off. "Wouldn't it make it worse for you if I lied like that? I don't want you punished for a crime you didn't commit. You didn't steal me or take me by force and I won't have you suffer for wanting to be with me as much as I want to be with you."

His chest expanded as he took a deep breath. "I will be punished regardless of if you came with me willing or not. If we're ever captured, you need to protect yourself from Volder's rage."

"How pissed could he be? Seriously? He doesn't even know me and he wasn't real happy about being stuck with a human. You should have seen his face when he first arrived at your house and you didn't hear the things he was saying."

A muscle in Rever's jaw jumped. "You don't understand Zorn men. If you say you went with me willingly it will enrage his pride. It will shame him to everyone, so to save his dignity, he would punish you harshly."

"The worst punishment for me would be to lose you. If that happens I won't care what happens to me."

Something softened in Rever's beautiful eyes. "I will care."

Her heart squeezed in her chest. Damn, the man could make her melt. The tenderness filling his gorgeous eyes made her love him deeper knowing he was more worried about her than himself. He'd given up so much already.

"Swear to me, my bound. Tell me for my peace that you will say I took you by force."

Tears welled in her eyes. "Don't make me promise something that I won't ever do. Please don't ask that of me because I never want to lie to you. There's no way that I would ever say you did something bad to me."

Rever's head lowered as he closed his eyes and their foreheads touched as he took a shaky breath. He lifted up an inch before his eyelids parted again and their gazes locked. His tongue slid across his lower lip while he studied her.

"I will just make sure that we are never captured then."

Her fingers explored his jawline, loving touching him. Her heart sped up when she became aware of Rever's state of arousal as he moved, shifting on her, feeling the firm press of his hard cock against her inner thigh. She wanted him again as much as he obviously wanted her. Not even hesitating, she wrapped her legs around his hips. Rever lifted up, letting her move under him into a better position. Their gazes remained locked.

"Make love to me."

She didn't have to ask twice before Rever's mouth lowered to hers. He was amazingly gentle as he positioned his bigger body over her smaller one, entering her at the same time that his mouth pressed to her lips. He caught her moan of pleasure between his lips, their tongues meeting as he pushed deeper inside her pussy.

Brenda's legs wrapped higher and tighter around his hips to give him freer access to move. Nothing had ever felt as wonderful as Rever did and it went beyond physical. His mouth left hers when he lifted his head, seating himself fully inside her body. A soft growl came from his parted lips.

"Tell me you love me. I want to hear it, Brenda."

"I'll always love you, Rever."

He withdrew a little before pushing back inside her body, pleasure transforming his features. He moved in slow movements, both of them enjoying every moment of his thick cock sliding inside her tight body. Her hands clutched at his broad, muscular shoulders as she gripped his hips tighter with her legs, moving against his body, trying to urge him to take her faster. His lips curved into a smile.

"You want more?"

She refused to look away from the sexiest eyes ever. "Yes."

He paused for a few heartbeats and then drove into her hard and fast. Ecstasy shot through her, a loud moan coming from her. "Yes!"

"Hold onto me."

She never wanted to let him go. Rever moved on her, his powerful body rippling as he used his strength to brace over her so he wouldn't crush her, his knees digging into the mattress for traction. His hips twisted slightly as he drove in and out of her in dominant thrusts. He was totally in control, totally masterful of her body, and she loved it as much as she did him.

Her inner muscles tightened as he worked her sensitive nerves. Growls and groans came from him but her moans were louder. Nothing had ever felt as amazing as Rever and she knew nothing ever would again. It was this man, this warrior, who had captured her heart with his soft ways, with his beautiful eyes and his complete abandonment of everything in his life just to be with her.

The climax hit her hard. Her gaze tore from his as her head was thrown back, her eyes squeezed shut as passion turned into total sexual bliss. Rever's body tensed and his movements slowed as he came. She felt him inside her while his cock pumped and jerked as he jetted his release deep into her.

They were both breathing hard when Rever stilled, caging her under his bigger frame. Opening her eyes Brenda met his, smiling.

"I love you and I want you to know how damn much, Rever. It's not just about the incredible sex but it's just you I adore."

The big Zorn shifted some of his weight, freeing one of his arms so he could cup her face with his hand. His fingers slid through her hair and lifted her head from the mat just a little bit. His gorgeous glowing blue eyes were mesmerizing.

"I have never felt for another woman what I feel for you. I have never experienced the emotion of love."

Her heart twisted. *Maybe one day he will fall in love with me. Maybe in time he —*

"Until I saw you. I was drawn to you like the pull of falling. There was no stopping or slowing where I landed. You are in my heart and are everything to me, my bound. I will die if I lose you and I will kill anyone who tries to take you from me. It tore me up inside when I had to take you to the medical center, wanting my offspring in your body to grow there knowing a part of us existed made from of the emotions we share. Life had lost the hold it had on me when I realized I could never keep you. I was ready to be miserable to save the family honor. I was raised as Argis and I've made sacrifices for our people always. It is what we do. You were one sacrifice I could not make, Brenda. Honor does not make my heart burst in my chest or make me shake with need to just be near it. You do. I have never felt love but I never had you in my arms. Now I have both."

She blinked back hot tears. "Oh, Rever." She held him tighter. "I love you so damn much. You're everything to me and I've never felt like this before either."

"We will have a good life but it won't be easy."

"I don't care how hard things will be in the Outlander area. As long as we're together I'll be so damn happy living in a cave with you."

He grinned. "Eventually Volder will bound to a woman and we can return. Tina is human and has a way of finding trouble so I am sure some unfortunate male will draw her attention. If he takes her to bed he will try to bound to her if he doesn't get to know her first."

Laughing, Brenda grinned at him. "I hope she doesn't open her mouth until after the sex."

He laughed. "That is how she tricked me. We barely exchanged words. The sex was —"

Brenda saw his shocked expression when her hand clamped over his mouth. His eyebrows rose as he stared down at her. She sighed, releasing his mouth.

"I don't want to hear how the sex was with her. Do you have any idea how much it killed me knowing you were touching her? I wanted you and it tore me up every night climbing into my bed on the other side of the house knowing you were with her."

His eyes narrowed. "There were no times for you to anguish over."

"I don't understand."

"After the day with the *killis* I couldn't stomach her touch. She was..." He frowned. "Not you. I had no desire to mount

125

her. I'm Zorn and I'm always in need of sex but it was your body I wanted to touch, you I wanted to sink into, and she was not you. I made her angry so she kicked me out of my bed. I slept on the floor and I took care of my own needs. I knew if I went to your room I would not leave your bed. I learned from taking you to medical how it tore me up to have to give you up and I knew I was never going to do that a second time. At night I lay thinking of what we shared, my body hurting with need for you. It was why I could not be around unless I had to be. My urges to touch you were too strong. I'm a warrior who battled his inner self, my Brenda."

She caressed his chest. "You never have to battle yourself again over me. If you want me, take me."

Rever smiled. "You will be sorry you say this. I long for you again. I will crave you over and over."

Arching her back, she wiggled her ass, and felt Rever was hard. The man didn't get soft when he was inside her. "So take me. I want you, Rever. I will always want you."

She closed her eyes when his lips lowered, wrapping her arms around his neck, and pulled him closer. A moan mingled between their tongues. Heaven was in his kiss and the way he made love to her. It was the last thought she had before she got lost in the intense pleasure their bodies created together.

Chapter Nine

&

It couldn't be happening, Brenda thought, gawking at the four large Zorn males surrounding her. They wore uniforms exactly the same as the border patrol ones she'd seen Rever wear. One of the men crouched down, staring into Brenda's terror-filled eyes. *This was not how I expected to wake up.*

"Get dressed now." His narrowed gaze swept over the thin blanket barely concealing her body. "Hurry."

She wondered where Rever was, her eyes scanning the room frantically. *Had these men hurt him? Wouldn't I have woken up if there had been a struggle?* A dim memory surfaced of Rever kissing her lips softly, telling her he was going hunting but it had been dark still in the cave. She was pretty sure that conversation and kiss from Rever really happened as her mind cleared of the sleep fog she was shaking off. Sunlight now streamed in from outside revealing it was definitely morning.

"If you don't dress we will take you out of here without clothing. You will be very uncomfortable, there are more males outside, and I don't want aroused males distracted by you."

"Where's Rever?" Brenda's voice shook with fear.

A deep growl tore from the man's parted lips. "We brought captured wild males with us to release them for him to run off to lure him far enough away from you so we could double back to rescue you."

She shook her head, her eyes pleading with the large Zorn warrior. "No. I don't want rescued. Rever saved me. I'm begging you to please just leave us alone. Don't take me from him."

The man's lips twisted into a grimace. "He broke the law by stealing a woman who doesn't belong to him. Get dressed or I will drag you out of here naked in front of dozens of males under my command outside. Do you want them to see you bare?" His gaze ran over her once more. "We are all curious what a human woman looks like without clothing but I doubt you would enjoy us examining you."

"Can you hand me clothes?" The last thing she wanted was for any of them to see her naked.

He turned his head, jerking it at one of his large men. That man turned, sniffed the area, and then stormed for Brenda's backpack that Rever had put in the corner. He bent, digging inside it, and a minute later he stormed back, tossing a shirt and a pair of pants at her. Brenda was grateful he'd chosen pants instead of one of those tunic-styled dresses since nothing went under them.

Keeping the cover in place, she awkwardly dressed under it. When she was in the clothes she pushed back the blanket. She looked around the cave again as she stood up, realizing that there was no escape. Two men were guarding the opening to the cave and the other two were now standing over her. She felt tiny compared to the tall men around her. She was caught and she knew it. Somewhere outside Rever was unaware of her predicament.

"Look," she stared at the one in charge, a black haired, bright green-eyed man. "Can we make a deal?"

Black eyebrows arched. "A deal?" His frown deepened.

"Just take me away and leave Rever alone. He was rescuing me if you know it or not. Please don't arrest him. I'll beg if you want. Just don't hurt him. He did it for me. I made him do it."

The man's gaze ran over her again, his eyelids narrowing. "I believe you could convince a smart man of anything, human. I am aware of your sexual appeal." Features hardened. "I won't be seduced by you. I am duty bound to take you back."

Shock tore through her. "I wasn't offering to seduce you. I wouldn't sleep with you." She was horrified he would think that. "Beg doesn't mean that on Earth. It means to plead with your sense of compassion. Do you have any of that?"

He shook his head. "I'm a warrior. Compassion is for fools and females." He turned his attention on the other man. "Shackle her but be gentle. She's fragile."

The other one gave a nod, moving behind Brenda. All she could do was tense when a large hand gripped her arm, pulling it behind her back. She knew there was no sense in her struggling, knowing these guys were too fast and strong to fight off. She turned her head, staring up at the man who pulled out a set of manacles akin to handcuffs only with thicker chains and wider wrist restraints while he hooked up her arms behind her back. His touch was gentle when he tested the manacles to make sure they weren't too tight on her wrists.

His coloring was unusual with silvery blond hair that was pulled back in a ponytail and fell mid way down his back. His eyes were an eerie silver-blue, which set him apart just as much as his skin did. He was not as deeply tanned as the others, his coloring more of a soft golden.

The man behind her stepped away. "Now we must trap Rever without a fight. No way do we want to kill an Argis."

The one in front of her nodded. "We'll use her to make him come peacefully. He won't fight knowing I am ready to kill her if he does."

Brenda fought back tears. *We had only had one night together. How in the hell did these assholes find us so quickly? These men are going to arrest Rever and he'll end up in a work camp while I'll be returned to Volder. No...*

Rever's words echoed in her head about lying if they were caught, knowing he was willing to sacrifice himself to protect her. To make matters worse, now these assholes were using her as bait to make Rever turn himself in without a fight. She knew he would do anything to protect her, even that. Her chin rose as she turned her head to glare up at the Zorn in charge.

"Rever did not steal me. Rever is completely innocent and had no choice but to bring me here. I'm confessing right now that I'm the guilty one who stole him."

The man's eyebrows arched again. "You stole him?" He actually threw back his head and a deep laugh rumbled out of him, looking highly amused as he stared at Brenda. "Tell me, tiny woman. How did you steal an Argis?"

Taking a deep breath, she tried to calm her pounding heart. She spotted Rever's gun-like weapon he'd had on him the night before. The guards they'd tricked at the supply building had seen it on Rever but maybe they wouldn't remember that little fact.

"Over there by the water is the weapon I used to point at Rever when I forced him from his home," she lied. "I told him that if I couldn't have him that I would blow up the *Drais* when Volder took me there if he didn't stay here with me. I'm human and I'm very cagey." She raised her chin higher, glaring at the man. "We're mean."

The one behind her laughed. "Watch out, Allot. She looks dangerous."

Allot was laughing still, his bright green gaze fixed on her and deep chuckles came from him. "You are mean?" He moved fast.

A gasp escaped from Brenda as the man's hands gripped her waist, lifting her off her feet and held her a few feet from his body. He raised her face level to him. He still looked damn amused but he'd stopped laughing.

"I could break you without pulling a muscle. You think I would believe this confession of yours? Don't insult my intelligence. You are pathetically weak as a human race and as a woman."

His hold on her wasn't painful but she didn't think he'd really hurt her. She was supposedly Volder's so she thought that hopefully meant Allot wouldn't kill her. She was afraid but she tried to hide it as she continued to glare at the man.

"The bigger they are, the harder they fall."

He cocked his head, staring at her. "I don't understand that saying."

Brenda brought her knee up firmly and quickly. She might not have hands since they were trapped behind her back but he'd lifted her high enough and close enough to his body that her knee hit dead on between his slightly parted thighs. She watched his face as his eyes went wide and the color drained from his normally tan face. She screamed out in terror when she was thrown away from him.

The other man with the silvery eyes caught her against his chest, saving her from a nasty fall to the floor. She hit him hard enough that it caused him to stagger back a few feet to keep hold of her without letting her fall. A tiny bit of sympathy welled inside her as Allot collapsed to his knees and gripped the front of his pants. Zorn warriors didn't wear sports cups but she bet he wished they did now. His head lowered, his black hair falling forward to obscure his face. The only sound he made was a hiss of air exhaling.

Regret filled Brenda. She probably shouldn't have done that but hell, he had been laughing at her when Rever's future was on the line. The man gripping her growled softly as he eased her down to her feet. His hands gripped the chains securing her wrists so she was tethered to him by them.

"I bet you think I'm mean now," she said softly. "Did that knee feel pathetically weak to you?"

In the blink of an eye the fallen man lifted his head up, sending his long hair flying backward as a snarl tore from his parted lips. His hands released his crotch and in a heartbeat he was on his feet. In two big steps he was in front of her to snarl again while he glared down into her frightened eyes, so close he nearly pressed against her body. He obviously recovered from that brutal of a hit faster than a human guy did.

"If you weren't a woman I'd kill you for that."

Her heart hammered hard in her chest. "I stole Rever and I forced him to take me. I told him I'd blow up the ship in space if he let that asshole Volder take me away. Rever is a hero for keeping me here and protecting your kind from my mean human temper."

"I can smell what happened here." Allot was still snarling when he spoke. "Did you force Argis to mount you as well?"

Brenda didn't look away from the furious, glowing green eyes. "I seduced him when I stripped naked—he's a man, after all. He fought the good fight but I wouldn't leave him alone. If I were naked rubbing against you and begged you to fuck me how long would you hold out?"

Green eyes narrowed. "Why don't we find out?" His glare lifted to the man behind her. "Release her, Coto."

Fear hit Brenda hard. "I'm not touching you."

The man who gripped her chain didn't let go. "Don't let your anger get to you, Allot. She belongs to another and she purposely provoked you."

"She injured me. She can make it better."

Coto jerked Brenda back against his body, growling. "You won't touch the alien. Admit she got the best of you. You insulted her and she retaliated so you are both guilty of provocation. She is not as weak or as pathetic as you deemed her. We have other matters to attend to right now like how Argis Rever will come soon. Do you want to explain to Hyvin Berrr how we allowed his son to be killed in battle? I don't."

A snarl tore from Allot. His rage-filled glare lowered to Brenda, narrowing dangerously. "I don't envy your future bound. He would be well to tie you up when you reach the *Drais*."

"If I end up with Volder he'd better. It's the only damn way he'll keep me."

"Let's go," Allot snarled when he spun on his boots and stormed for the cave opening.

Coto kept his voice low when he spoke. "I admire your courage but that was not smart, alien female. Allot has a long memory with a short temper. It is a long way back to the border so stay close to me so I can make sure he doesn't hurt you."

Looking up as she turned her head, Brenda frowned at the man over her shoulder. "What do you care? You don't even know me."

He gave a nod. The man had the strangest silvery blue glowing eyes but they were really pretty. His black eyelashes clashed with the silver-shaded blond hair he had but it made him look exotic and almost reminded her of a guy at home who wore eyeliner and mascara in high school. He'd had amazing eyes too thanks to hitting his mother's makeup. This guy was naturally that way. The combination of his looks made him appear almost Goth in a muscled, buffed-up way.

"You are correct. I don't know you. I do however know Rever and all of his brothers because I was raised with them. My father was killed when I was young and Hyvin Berrr took me into their home, raising me as a son not of his blood. For Rever to steal you he must care greatly for you. I am trying to protect the woman he threw his life away for."

Shock tore through Brenda. "Then why are you here? Why are you hunting him?"

The large Zorn hesitated. "I came to make sure he was not killed. Some would love to bring down an Argis regardless of the personal price such an action would cost them. Hyvin Berrr would kill any man who harmed his blood. Let's go. Do as you are told so that I may protect you and Rever. We are working on a plan to clear this mess up but we can't do that if both of you are dead."

Hope soared. "So you think we can get around this law?"

Shaking his head, Coto gently pushed her forward. "Rever can't keep you but we can get the charges dropped against him. You weren't bound to Volder yet so he won't be able to claim years of Rever's life for mounting a bound mate. Hyvin believes he can get Rever out of this mess."

Her hope was crushed instantly with his words. The only comfort she had as she was led out of the cave was that at least Rever wouldn't end up in a work camp. Sunlight blinded her for a few blinks until she adjusted to the red-tinged brightness. She was shocked by the dozens of Zorn men waiting outside in their matching uniforms.

Allot glared at Brenda for long seconds before his focus shifted to Coto. "Stand there on high ground with her. Argis will be along shortly and I want him to have a clear view that we have her." He turned his attention away to face the men he led. "Stay back if he charges for the woman. We are under orders to capture but to not harm him."

One of the men snorted. "Of course not. He's Argis."

Allot snarled, showing sharp teeth. "Watch what you say."

The man dropped his gaze, giving a short jerk of his head, his head bowing. "Of course."

"No weapons," Allot ordered. His body tensed as his head turned, sniffing the wind. "He comes."

Brenda saw Rever walk out from behind one of the boulders to the right of her down the slope looking furious. He stopped walking.

"Argis," Allot bowed his head. "We're under orders from your father to take you back. He has made his wishes clear that you are to come with us peacefully."

Rever snarled. "Let her go and leave us."

Allot met Rever's glare from across the distance. "If you attack we have permission to kill the alien."

"My father wouldn't allow that," Rever snarled.

"He didn't," Coto said loudly. "She belongs to Volder under the law and he was the one who gave the order to kill her." Disgust was clear in his voice when he'd spoken. "Do what your father says, Argis Rever. Your father is a wise man who knows what he is ordering."

Fury gripped Rever's expression. "I know where his thoughts lay. She's mine now that I bound to her and I won't give her up."

Allot snarled. "You already have an alien. You can't bound with two. Not even an Argis has that privilege."

Rever took a slow step forward and didn't look at the nearly three dozen Zorn warriors. His attention fixed on Allot. "I challenge you a fight for her."

Shock paled Allot's face. "She's not mine to challenge over so I won't fight you."

Rever moved so fast that it shocked Brenda. He leapt a good five feet to the boulder he'd moved closest to and landed on all fours. His powerful body was tense as he straightened up, slowly standing from a crouch, and his electric blue eyes burned with rage as he glared at Allot again.

"Release her or die, Allot. Those are the options I am giving you. If her life is extinguished, everyone here dies with her. I will fight to my last breath. I won't allow you to take my woman away from me to give another male."

Brenda was terrified for his life, knowing Rever was going to get killed over her. Hot tears filled her eyes. "Rever, please don't die for me." Her voice shook. "I couldn't live with that and if you die, I die."

His mouth compressed into a tight line as his gorgeous blue gaze locked with her tear-filled eyes. "Are you mine, Brenda?"

"Always."

Rever responded with a roar that tore through the area, loud enough to hurt Brenda's ears. He leapt again, his powerful body landed in a roll in the dirt at the bottom of the slope but when he came up to his feet, he moved at full speed. Brenda could only suck in air as Rever launched himself at

Allot. The other man barely had time to tense before Rever attacked.

The first punch Rever threw made Allot stagger backward with a loud groan. Allot caught his balance, snarling, before he threw out a fist too. Rever ducked it, missed the intended blow, and threw himself forward to hit shoulder first into Allot's body. Both of them went down.

Men rushed forward but Coto stopped them. "No! Back off," he snarled. "Let them fight."

The men slowly retreated to a safe distance but some of them didn't look happy about it, a few obviously outright pissed off. Brenda's terrified gaze flew to the two men on the ground where red dirt clouded up around them. Rever and Allot exchanged heavy punches, rolled around and fought for control of the other. Rever ended up on top, his fist slamming into the other man's face. Rever climbed to his feet after Allot was unconscious. He turned, facing the group of men with a roar that exploded out of his open mouth. He took a fighting stance.

"Enough, Argis," Coto growled. "You don't want to do this."

Rever turned his head to stare at the Zorn who had spoken. His uniform was split in a few places from the fight, his tan skin showed near his shoulder, and across his stomach where the material had been torn open. He showed teeth as he growled and his beautiful eyes were furious while he glared at Coto.

"Let my woman go."

Behind her, Brenda heard Coto take a deep breath. She tried to walk toward Rever but the warrior gripped her chain tighter, jerking her back hard enough that she stumbled and bumped into his chest.

"Now," Coto snarled.

In shock and horror, Brenda saw some of the men raise weapons that resembled guns at Rever. He must have seen their movements out of the corner of his vision, his head jerked in their direction where they were grouped together, and a roar tore from him when the men fired at him.

Brenda screamed, seeing Rever stagger as he was shot. She went wild, twisted hard against the restraints and screamed again when the man she loved dropped to his knees. Rever turned his head to look at Brenda. She couldn't look away as she saw his eyes roll up into his head so just the whites of them showed. Almost in slow motion his body swayed before he crumpled hard on the red dirt packed ground.

Coto snarled in anger and the hold on Brenda was suddenly gone. She didn't mentally tell herself to do it but just instinctively rushed for Rever. When she reached him, she stumbled, off balance with her hands bound behind her back, and just dropped to her knees to frantically look for bloody wounds on his still body.

His uniform was black but she didn't see any wetness to indicate that he was bleeding where she saw things sticking out of him. They appeared to be yellow round pellets that had barely embedded just in his skin and uniform. She fought the restraints but she couldn't break free.

"Rever?" Tears blinded her, thinking they'd killed him over her. "REVER!" She cried out his name when she bent over him, staring at his handsome face.

His eyes remained closed but she did see his chest rise and fall, assuring her that he wasn't dead. He'd collapsed to the side but he'd landed on his back and he wasn't trying to get up. She turned her head to stare in horror at Coto.

"How could you? Help him, damn it. Get him a doctor!"

Coto slowly walked forward. "He will live."

"You had him shot!" She screamed the words, struggling to get to her feet but couldn't find the balance to do it. All she could do was glare up at Coto. She wanted to launch herself at the bastard to kill him. "I thought you said you were raised with him."

The Zorn man stopped a few feet back. "Those are sleep pellets that will keep him unconscious for a few hours. I would never have him harmed."

Relief poured through Brenda that Rever wasn't seriously hurt and dying. She swiveled her head back, staring down at the man she was in love with to assure herself that he was breathing but unconscious. She bent over him more, needing to touch him. With her hands held behind her back she lost her balance and pitched forward to land across Rever's chest, her face was just inches from his.

"Rever, I'm so sorry," she whispered. "I love you."

Brenda put her face in his neck, feeling his strong heartbeat against her lips when she pressed them to the skin just under his ear. She inhaled his wonderful scent even though he smelled strongly of dirt and sweat from his fight. She didn't care. With every breath he took it moved her body sprawled on his chest.

She screamed out in protest when Coto bent down and grabbed her to take her away from Rever. He wrapped one arm around her chest while he gripped her around her waist with his other arm and totally lifted her off Rever's still form. She screamed again, kicking wildly at Coto's legs but he just spread them apart to make it harder for her to nail him with her bare feet. He held her tightly in his arms and kept her from touching the ground while he addressed his men.

"Gently restrain him and don't mark him up like we do the wild ones." Coto's voice was harsh with anger as he spoke. "I want him loaded and carefully watched but let's hurry. I want to be back across the border by the time he wakes."

One of the men was crouched by Allot. "He's alive but he's seriously injured. His jaw is broken and I think his shoulder is dislocated."

Coto sighed. "Shoot him with the sleeping pellets to keep him out so he doesn't suffer from his injures until medical can fix him."

Coto started walking, still carrying Brenda in his arms where she dangled down the front of his body. She turned her head to glare up at him.

"Traitor."

He frowned. "I don't know this word."

"Asshole. Do you know that one? You're a total asshole for betraying Rever like this. Do you know what I'm saying now?"

Coto shook his head and just kept walking. "I did this to save his life. Volder wanted to bring his men into the hunt for both of you. He has highly skilled warriors under his control and he would have made sure Rever died. I knew I had to lead Allot to where I knew Rever would go so we made it to him first. Now be silent."

Shock tore through her quickly, followed by rage as she stared up at the man over her shoulder. "You told them how to find us?"

"I knew this was where I would take you if I had stolen a woman. It was a comfortable place to raise a family in the Outlander area that Rever could easily defend. We have been here many times together. I knew, yes, that he would be here. We are very close like brothers."

"You son of a bitch. And you betray him still? How could you?"

An angry growl tore from Coto. He stopped abruptly and almost dropped Brenda on her feet but he eased her down gently at the last second. He spun her around to make her face him while he gripped her arms just above her elbows. His eyelids narrowed dangerously, rage fixed on his tense features.

"I saved him. Did you hear me when I said Volder was going to send his warriors to the Outlander area to hunt for you both? He would have made sure Rever died for stealing his future bound. That is a killing offense on Zorn if it is not brought before a judge. I had to reach Rever first to capture him to keep him alive. He is my brother in all ways but blood and he is my closest friend."

"Maybe Volder and his men wouldn't have found us. Did you ever think of that? He was in a big hurry to get back to his ship so how much time could he have wasted looking for us? He would have given up really soon if he couldn't have found us to go back to the *Drais*. Rever and I could have had a future together out here."

Regret shone in the large man's strange blue eyes. "It was a chance Hyvin Berrr and I were not willing to take with Rever's life at stake. Volder has many warriors under his command who Rever trained when they were young so some of them could have known about this place. We were not willing to take the risk."

Some of her anger left her. "We love each other. Do you understand that? I don't want to be with Volder. Rever and I belong together."

The man nodded, misery etched on his features. "Rever obviously is obsessed with you. He left his honor behind, brought shame to his family to be with you but he is bound to another. I am sorry but Zorn law forbids your union. There is nothing to do except save Rever's life. Even if he must pay by working the harshest camp he will live and you will live. Volder will be angry but he still has honor and it is not admirable to kill women on Zorn. If you love Rever you must put his life over your own happiness and not make this harder for him by resisting the destiny you both must face apart."

Pain tore through her. She turned her head away from Coto so he wouldn't see her tears that fell as she watched four men gently lift the unconscious Rever by each of his limbs. They slowly carried his limp body toward a set of large boulders.

"Where are they taking him?"

"We have vehicles waiting that are hidden from sight of this place or we never would have been able to sneak up on him. I was surprised we got this close but you obviously distract Rever. Releasing the wild males, we had captured near here was my idea knowing he'd protect you by chasing them away. It gave us the opportunity to sneak in from the opposite direction to reach you. Saving Rever's life is my top priority. If you truly love him then our mission is the same."

Brenda turned her head, looking up at the big Zorn, and saw real regret in his silvery blue eyes. "You suck."

He frowned. "I suck what?"

Frustration welled in her. It was hard to insult Zorn people when they didn't get half of what she said. "Forget it. I don't like what you did. I just..." Pain tore through her as she watched Rever be carried from her sight. "I just want to be with him."

"I'm sorry." The large Zorn warrior gently gripped her arm. "We must go."

Chapter Ten

&

Fear filled Brenda as she met the furious eyes of the Zorn leader and Hyvin Berrr was definitely pissed off. His muscles bulged on his arms, which were clearly revealed in the tight sleeveless shirt he wore. Her gaze drifted lower to glance at what looked similar to pirate breeches. Sweat beaded his buffed up body making it obvious that he'd been working out or doing something physically challenging. When he spun away, pacing in the large chamber she was led to, she saw his hair was pulled back with a leather strap in a ponytail that fell down his back to his ass.

Memories hit her of the last time she'd seen the Zorn leader a week before when he'd sent her to Rever's home. It seemed to her as if more time than that had passed, almost a lifetime ago, and now she was standing before him again waiting for him to tell her what was going to happen to her.

"He will be fine," Coto said softly to the Zorn leader. "He did not become alert on the return trip. They restrained him so when he wakes he won't be able to fight."

Hyvin Berrr turned, sharp teeth showing as his mouth opened, and a growl tore from his throat. "My son is being charged with stealing a woman." The man's glare fixed on Brenda. "This is your fault, woman. My son has lost his reason after your body taunted him."

"Are you joking?" She frowned at the man. "Have you seen Tina? She's the one with the body. I'm…" She swallowed as the man's face darkened with rage, letting her know he was really ticked off and she seemed to be pissing him off more. "I'm not as attractive as her. This has nothing to do with my body. We love each other."

142

The leader snarled and spun away again, pacing the large room. Coto looked miserable as he watched the other man.

Coto took a deep breath. "I know this is bad, Father. I know what Rever did was insanity but he loves her."

Hyvin Berrr growled. "I know this like I know Rever and he had to feel very strongly for her to take her to the Outlander area." He stopped pacing and slowly turned to meet Coto's eyes. "What do I do? I must follow the law even though it is my own offspring. I will lose respect if I don't and a leader without that is no leader at all. I can have the charges dropped but he will never forgive me for handing over his woman to another warrior. He will hunt down Volder and kill him to reclaim her."

Shock tore through Brenda. *Will Rever come after me?* Part of her rejoiced and then part of her was frightened. Logic told her that if he came after her it could get Rever killed. Volder lived on a spaceship with warriors under his command and Rever would have to go on that ship to get her since she knew that's where Volder would take her to live.

"He would not," Coto shook his head. "It would be a battle he could not win."

"He won't see it that way." The Zorn leader looked miserable. "I know he will fight to the death for his woman because I would do the same and he is much like me. If I had a woman who gripped my heart that tightly I would do anything to keep her." Sadness flashed in his eyes. "I have no answer this time."

The chamber doors opened, startling Brenda. Dread hit her as she turned her head, hoping it wasn't Volder. The tall Zorn woman who walked into the room was almost as muscular as one of the males and seeing her stunned Brenda. The Zorn was dressed as if she were a man in leather tight pants and a tight male shirt that revealed she wasn't wearing a bra since her breasts swayed as she marched forward. Her hair was cut to her shoulders, another oddity since all the Zorn women had long hair, and then the strange woman fixed her furious attention directly on Hyvin Berrr.

"I was informed Rever was returned." The woman stormed right up to Hyvin Berrr, glaring at him. "I won't be humiliated by having your son work in some camp like a criminal, Berrr." The woman twisted her head, a pair of almost black eyes turning on Brenda.

Shaken by the amount of rage directed at her, Brenda took a step back, feeling the Zorn's hatred almost as if it were a physical blow. The woman's face was a little harsh and definitely cold. A growl came from the woman, her sharp teeth showing as her eyelids narrowed.

"You are what my son threw his pride away for?" Disgust showed on her features. "If you are dead you can't be the object of our shame any longer." She moved, coming at Brenda.

Horror hit Brenda the second she understood the woman was going to kill her. She didn't know why but the woman definitely had the look of murder in her cold, evil-looking dark eyes. Brenda backed up and almost stumbled over Coto's foot in the process of getting out of the other woman's way. Coto moved to block the advancing woman from reaching her.

Hyvin Berrr moved too, he lunged forward to grab the woman's arm and spun her around as he halted her. "No, Alluwn. Rever loves her."

"Love?" The woman hissed. "That is for fools and weak females."

Sadness flashed over the Zorn leader's face. "I am aware of your opinion of emotions. He is your son and he would hate you even more if you were to attack his woman." He paused. "I won't allow it."

Shock tore through Brenda, her mouth dropping open. *That was Hyvin Berrr's bound? That woman is Rever's mother? Rever definitely takes after his father in looks.* The woman was glaring at Hyvin Berrr as if she were ready to kill him. If he wasn't gripping both of her arms Brenda wondered if the Zorn woman would have hit him or at least tried to. Brenda pressed her lips together.

The woman moved, pushing against the man's larger body, going almost nose to nose with him. "Do you think I care? They are your sons and I won't live with the shame caused by one of them due to his lack of control. Aliens are fine to mount but he stole that one, abandoned his bound, and now I look weak. They will think I raised a warrior without self-control."

He snorted. "No one would accuse you of that. Your brutality is well known, my bound."

Alluwn hissed. "You will stop the shame and kill the alien to be done with it."

"I won't and you don't give me orders."

The couple glared at each other but Alluwn finally lowered her eyes. "What are you going to do about this?"

"I am deciding," Hyvin Berrr said quietly.

"There is nothing to decide. If you won't kill the pathetic alien then send her off the planet with the warrior who wants her. He commands the *Drais*, correct?"

"Yes."

"Then send her off our world to be rid of her and I will handle Rever."

Hyvin Berrr growled. "You will stay away from my son. Don't you have some male to go bend for?"

Alluwn hissed. "I don't allow males to mount me. I mount them."

He gave her a shove. "Then go and never come here again. You made your choice. We are bound until death because I made a vow but you made one as well. Stay away from my sons. You have no right to come here to demand anything."

The woman growled and shot Brenda a murderous look. Her angry focus shifted to Coto and a cold smile curved on her lips. "Hello, Coto. Why don't you come give your second mother a kiss?"

Coto looked pissed off as he growled. "No."

Hyvin Berrr snarled. "Leave now."

The woman turned her head, still smiling coldly. "Don't you want to watch a man being mounted by me? I always wanted Coto but he wouldn't touch me. He feels that useless emotional bond to you for taking him into our home. It is pathetic for a true warrior to allow emotion to rule his physical self. Watching me taking a male is the closest you will ever come seeing my body that way again. I know how good it feels for you to release your seed into a woman. Does it hurt when you remember what that was like? Do you burn with the desire to feel it again?"

Two massive arms crossed over his chest as Hyvin Berrr's blue eyes turned ice cold. "If it is you then I don't hurt or burn with desire to release myself into a woman."

Rage filled her features. "Make sure this mess is fixed. Do your duty by me."

"Always," he snarled.

Alluwn stormed out of the room and slammed the massive door closed behind her. Coto released Brenda to take a step closer to Hyvin Berr but then halted. He watched the other man with concern.

"It is not your fault she is like that."

The Zorn leader nodded slowly. "I'm aware. What are your suggestions?"

"I don't know what to do either, Father. I am failing you."

Hyvin Berrr walked forward to put his large hand on Coto's shoulder. "You could never fail me. I am always proud of you and remember you saved Rever's life today. They will arrive soon and when they do, we will deal with this together."

Coto reached up, his hand gripping the other man's shoulder. "Together we stand."

"Together we stand." Hyvin Berrr repeated.

Both men released each other when the doors opened again and in unison they turned to face whoever walked in. Brenda twisted around to look too and felt instant dread when Volder and five males dressed in the same uniforms stormed into the room. Volder's gaze sought out Brenda immediately, clear fury poured from his dark eyes all directed at her. He snarled, coming at Brenda fast and with ferocity.

Hyvin Berrr moved to step between Brenda and the advancing Volder. "Hold," he ordered.

Volder stopped to bow his head. "Hyvin Berrr."

"Your promised bound has been retrieved." Hyvin Berrr sounded irritated. "The others will arrive any time."

Volder's head snapped up and his dark stare locked on Hyvin Berrr. "I demand a challenge."

"Denied."

Shock gripped Volder's features. "I know he is your son but he stole my woman."

"She is not yours yet. You have not bound to her."

"He emptied his seed in her, did he not? She could be with his offspring now that he stole her from me." Volder was snarling. "It is a great insult to my pride if I have to raise his blood as my own."

Hyvin Berrr snarled back. "Do you dare say raising a blood offspring of mine would be less than an honor for you?"

Whatever answer Volder was going to say was lost as the chamber doors opened again to allow a lot of Zorn men to walk into the room. There had to be fifty of them who filed silently in and the number of them stunned Brenda. They stood by the walls, surrounding Brenda and the men already present. A group of red-clad Zorn men came in last as they led a heavily chained Rever in, each of the half dozen red-uniformed men held the leads of his chains that acted as leashes.

Brenda blinked back tears as she met Rever's gaze after taking note of his wet hair that let her know they'd had him shower. He was almost naked and only covered in loose black shorts. They had chained him by all four limbs and there a thick metal collar locked around his throat. She saw rage burn in Rever's eyes as they stared at each other but she knew it wasn't directed at her. He looked away from Brenda finally to stare at his father.

"I demand to challenge Volder for my woman."

Volder snarled. "Your woman? She is mine! I accept your challenge to the death."

"Enough!" Hyvin Berrr roared the word. "A challenge is denied. We will do this according to the laws. That is my final word. We follow the law."

A Zorn man stepped forward. "May I lead the judgment, Hyvin Berrr?"

Nodding, Hyvin Berrr stepped to the center of the room. "You have the floor, Zalk."

Zalk looked about seventy years old and was older than any of the other males within sight. White streaked his black hair, making him appear striking with the two-toned long mane. He moved to stand next to the Zorn leader.

"I am judge. Bring forth the case. I am willing to listen and give my verdict."

The doors opened again and a man walked in who Brenda turned to study, recognizing Rever's brother instantly from the strong family resemblance. As he marched forward she took note of the border guard uniform he wore. He looked a few years younger than Rever when he got close enough to get a better look at. Electric blue eyes identical to Rever's met hers for just a second before he jerked his gaze away to his father, bowing his head as he stepped next to Coto.

"I apologize for my lateness but I was just informed of the situation."

Zalk nodded. "It is good to see you, Vhon."

Coto frowned, shooting a glare at the man next to him. "What are you doing here?" he whispered.

"Saving Rever's ass," Vhon whispered back.

"Don't," Coto warned. "Be silent."

"You." Vhon smiled. "I know what I am doing."

Coto groaned softly, a look of distaste on his features.

"Bring forth the dispute," Zalk said loudly.

Rever didn't resist when the guards brought him to the center of the room. He glanced at Brenda again as they led him past her. She took a step in his direction but Coto gripped her arm and jerked her back. Rever turned his head and his gaze remained on her while he was led to stand next to his father.

"Release him," Hyvin Berrr ordered the guards. "He will behave in my chambers."

"What is going on?" Brenda whispered. "Who are all of these men?"

Coto inched closer, almost touching her arm. "They are judges from the districts here to witness what happens. It is our way." He kept his voice soft. "They represent all of Zorn and are here to make sure the laws are followed. Zalk is the top judge of all judges and he is also Hyvin Berrr's council."

"I will hear the dispute," Zalk said loudly again when Volder stepped forward.

Brenda noticed Rever was still chained but his guards released the lines so he walked, dragging the chains behind him. Only feet separated Rever from Volder when they each faced the judge. Both men studied each other. Even from ten feet away Brenda could feel to animosity between both Zorn males.

"Look at me," Zalk snapped.

Both men complied and Brenda's heart pounded with fear for Rever. *What if they did sentence him to some work camp? How bad were they? They didn't sound as though they would be fun and Zorn warriors are tough guys, almost brutal at times.* She was sure something titled a work camp would be difficult.

"If I may," Hyvin Berrr stated. "I have a fact to add."

Zalk nodded. "Present."

Hyvin called forth the men who had been with Volder at Rever's house. Brenda listened to Hyvin order them to recount what happened and how Volder had treated her. She sensed eyes on her but she didn't look around at all those Zorn men, not wanting to acknowledge them. She felt damn uncomfortable being the only female in a room full of huge, alien men. She wasn't afraid for her safety but as the details of her being stripped came out, she felt a blush heat her cheeks.

Hyvin Berrr stepped back. "I ordered Rever to put the human under his protection and he believed that Volder's behavior was abusive. Rever, did you feel that the human woman was safe in Volder's care?"

"No," Rever growled. He turned his head to glower at Volder. "I did not. He doesn't deserve her."

"You do?" Volder snarled. "You mounted her, did you not? You have a bound human already and yet you took mine."

Rever opened his mouth, showing teeth, and growled low. "I mounted her and emptied my seed in her many times. She is mine."

They snarled at each other.

Zalk roared. "Enough. Hold. You will control your tempers now."

Both men looked ready to fight but neither moved.

Zalk gave a sharp nod. "The law is clear. The human woman will be given to Volder but the charges against Rever are dropped. He feared for the safety of the alien." Zalk glared at Volder. "You will treat the alien with all honors given to a bound Zorn woman. You will—"

"Never keep my woman," Rever snarled. "I will come for her if you take her from me. We will settle this off Zorn where the law does not apply."

"I look forward to it," Volder sneered. "While you find transport to my ship I will mount her over and over."

Rever roared, lunging at Volder. The guards moved fast, separating the enraged men. Rever's chains were held by six men while another six surrounded Volder to keep him in place a good ten feet from where Rever was held. Both men glared at each other.

"Touch my bound and you will die painfully." It was a promise and a threat issued by Rever. "One bruise on my woman, if I even scent fear on her, you will pay with blood and pain like you have never known."

"She is promised to me!" Volder thumped his chest with his fist. "She was bound to my brother so by right she is mine."

"Finally!" Vhon moved suddenly. "I demand to present facts," he said loudly.

Everyone turned to look at the tall male. Brenda saw Hyvin Berrr's face and he looked pissed off. "Stop, Vhon. This is a law meeting. This is no time for your pranks."

Vhon's shoulders straightened, staring at his father while his lips pressed into a tight line. He looked away to focus on the judge. "Zalk, I demand to present facts. It will change your ruling. I was waiting for Volder to state the human was bound to his brother and now that he has, I am disputing his claim."

Zalk gave a nod. "Present the proof."

Lips spread into a wide grin as Vhon turned to face Brenda. She was stunned when the man stared directly at her. He winked—his eyes were identical to Rever's—a gesture she'd never expected from a Zorn.

"Did Valho mount you, human? Did he plant his seed inside your body?"

Brenda felt her face flame and swore she could feel every male eye in the room on her while they waited for her to tell them if she had sex with Valho. She shook her head.

"Be clear," Rever's younger brother ordered her. "Speak louder so all may hear."

"No," she said loudly. "He was giving me time to adjust to him but he was killed before we ever had sex."

Vhon turned around to grin at Zalk. "I state the fact that Volder has no claim on the human since a bounding to his brother never took place. She was unbound and therefore free to choose for herself which male to be with."

Volder snarled. "Valho took her with intent from her planet after she agreed to bound to him. She has admitted that. Bound or not I have the right to her."

Brenda silently pleaded with the older Zorn judge to look at her and see how badly she wished he'd rule that Volder had no claim. That would solve everything. Hope flared inside her that the nightmare was about to end.

"He has a good point," Hyvin Berrr said quickly. "The bounding was not completed."

Zalk refused to even glance at Brenda, completely ignored her as he seemed to contemplate the matter for a long minute. He took a deep breath. Brenda held hers, her heart pounding in her chest.

"The human agreed to bound, the law is clear and I rule Volder has a claim on her."

Slumping with disappointment, Brenda blinked back tears, her hope dashed. *It isn't fair, damn it.* Hyvin Berrr looked pissed off but he didn't speak. Brenda looked at Rever seeing the furious glower he shot at the older judge. Volder was the only one who appeared pleased with the ruling.

Vhon turned his head, staring down the aisle. "Allow them inside," he called out to the men on the opposite end of it. "My other facts to present are out there."

Brenda had to shift to the left a little to see the door when it opened and wondered what other plan Rever's younger brother had come up with to try to help them. He was trying and she prayed whatever else he wanted to introduce into the court proceeding would make Zalk change his mind.

She watched two more of Rever's relatives come forward, one of them was Ral, the brother she'd met. The other man was almost a replica of Ral and Rever, obviously another brother. A terrified-looking uniformed Zorn male was being hauled in by Ral who held the Zorn by his arm and the back of his neck. The other brother was gripping a highly annoyed Tina by her arm.

"What is the meaning of this?" Volder yelled. "This isn't fair if the facts being spoken come from his blood. They will lie to help him win."

Brenda recognized the uniformed Zorn being pushed forward as one of Rever's guards from his house when they drew close enough for her to get a good look at him. Ral forced the guard closer and then stopped him.

Ral looked furious. "You dare accuse me of telling a falsehood? You don't even know why we are here or what is to be said, Volder. I am Argis Ral, a judge, and my honor is never in question. Speak of it again and we will fight."

"Enough," Zalk ordered. "Present, Argis Ral. Your honor is not an issue. Proceed."

"Talk," Ral ordered the guard, forcing the Zorn to his knees before Zalk. "Tell him the truth now."

The petrified guard refused to look at Rever. His mouth opened but nothing came out. He visibly swallowed hard, muscles working in his throat. His mouth opened again. "I plead forgiveness, Argis Rever. She teased me until I couldn't resist her. She—"

"Shut up, you idiot," Tina snapped.

Rever frowned, studying the guard for a long minute before his interest shifted to Tina. She glared at Rever with her arms crossed over her chest but she was looking a little paler than usual.

"Don't look at me like that," Tina snapped. "This is your damn fault. You fuck me, drag me to this backward-ass planet, and the only damn conversations we have are about how you want to mount me like I'm a damn animal. You're the dog, not me. All you wanted was to fuck me over and over. I'm a woman with needs that you didn't meet. I like talking and we've got nothing in common."

Rever's eyes narrowed but he didn't say a word. Brenda was thinking up some words to say. She opened her mouth to tell Tina what a bitch she was but Coto gripped her shoulder, shaking his head no at her when she looked up at him. She frowned but closed her mouth, holding still. Her attention returned to the center of the room.

"I confess," the guard on his knees growled. "I allowed the human to mount me. She took me inside her body and it felt so good I could not bring myself to lift her off my lap. I spread my seed into her body."

The room went eerie silent. Brenda saw shock on many faces when she glanced around the room. She wasn't surprised in the least that Tina had screwed the guard. She looked at Rever to see his reaction. He actually smiled as his gaze met Brenda's. *This is really good news that Tina is a slut judging by Rever's reaction*, she thought. Brenda bit her lip, waiting to see what would happen and hoping that something good was going to come out of this revelation.

"She broke the bounding agreement first," Ral said softly. "Tell Zalk when you allowed the human your seed."

The guard was staring at Rever and he looked confused. "It was the first day that Argis Rever returned to work. I had guard duty in the backyard and she came out, dropped her clothing, and went to her knees before me taking me inside her mouth. I couldn't tell her no when she ordered me to lie down for her. I wanted her." He paused. "My regret, Argis Rever. I have shamed my family and I have shamed my service to you.

I deserve the harshest death but I plead for quickness on the condition of no fight."

Brenda wondered what the hell that meant, totally confused. Coto leaned down. "It's a death sentence to mount someone's bound. They fight to the death. The younger male knows Rever will make him suffer for hours if he wishes to take his time killing him. He is offering to not fight back if Rever will just snap his neck quickly."

Rever took a step toward the kneeling guard. The frightened Zorn lifted his head, his eyes closing. The men holding Rever's chains released him so he could walk to the other man. Brenda opened her mouth to ask Rever to not kill the guy but before she could say a word, Rever spoke.

"I won't kill you, Olt. I punish you worse by not offering a challenge and giving you Tina. I concede my bound to you. Take the Earth woman and go freely."

"What?" Tina screeched. She glared at Rever. "You can't give me to him. He's nobody. He was just fun to fuck a few times and he's not even that good at it. I just did it to get even with you since you were hot and bothered over that fat-assed freeloader you let stay in our house. I saw the way you looked at her."

Rever was still grinning. "Zorn law, Tina. You offered your body to another male and you let him spread his seed inside you so you belong to him now."

Zalk gave a nod of his head. "The law requires the males to challenge for a bound and Rever has conceded. You are now bound to Olt. Go now with your bound." Zalk issued the order to the shocked guard. "Take your bound away now, Olt. Go and know gratitude of Argis Rever's generosity since all are well aware that you would have died in a challenge."

"No damn way," Tina tried to fight her way to Rever but his brother kept a good grip on her arm so she couldn't get near him. "Rever, damn you. Don't let him take me anywhere.

You brought me to this God-forsaken planet. You can't just give me away like a damn puppy. You're the fucking animal."

Rever crossed his arms over his chest. "He will cherish you." His grin was still wide. "The next male you offer yourself to be aware that if you are as pleasant to Olt as you were to me, he will give you away when the male challenges for you. Have a happy life." He grinned at his brother. "Hand her over, Argernon. She has a new bound."

The brother, Argernon, who kept hold of Tina, grinned back at Rever. "I am happy to hand her over."

Olt quickly rose to his feet still looking stunned but also relieved that he wasn't being killed. He moved fast for Tina. Tina glared up at the large guard.

"No. I'm not yours."

Olt growled. "Come now."

Tina glared. "No fucking way. It was just a few quick fucks. I am not going anywhere with you."

Argernon released Tina. "Take her and go quickly. She's yours."

Olt moved fast. Brenda watched as the man bent, grabbing Tina, and tossed the protesting woman over his shoulder. His large hand slapped her ass hard when she tried to wiggle off his shoulder. His other arm locked over the back of her thighs to hold her in place. He strode quickly for the doors.

Brenda couldn't help but smile as she watched Tina being taken away. One of the Zorn warriors opened the door for Olt. Everyone in the room could hear Tina screaming at the "big ox" to put her down until they left the large chamber and the door was firmly closed again.

Brenda's attention flew to Rever to find him watching her with a smile. She wondered what was going to happen now, almost afraid to hope for a good resolution.

Rever turned away, taking his focus from her. He nodded at his brother Ral, another nod to his brother Argernon, and then shot a grin to his brother, Vhon. Vhon laughed. Rever gave his attention back to Zalk.

"With respect of the new facts, I now offer challenge for the human to Volder."

Excitement and dread raced through Brenda when the reality of the situation became clear as if a ton of bricks had fallen on her. It sank in that Rever wasn't legally bound to Tina anymore and it was no wonder he was so happy that Tina was someone else's problem. He'd have to fight to win Brenda now and she was afraid over the possibility of him getting hurt or killed.

Zalk stared at Rever for a long moment. He turned his head and eyed Volder. "He will kill you, Volder. The human is unknown to you and she obviously prefers Argis Rever." He paused. "Do you accept the challenge? There is no lost pride to concede under these circumstances."

Volder snarled. "I accept the challenge to the death."

Brenda's knees almost crumpled. *They are going to fight to the death and Rever can be killed. He could die trying to win me.* She reacted by kicking at Coto, her foot making contact with his shin as she jerked hard at her arm he held, managing to catch him by surprise. He stumbled, releasing her. Rever turned around right as she threw herself at him.

Rever's arms went around her to hold her in his arms. She felt heavy chains running down her back from his wrists and the other chain was between their bodies where it hung from the collar around his throat. She didn't care about how uncomfortable that chain was against her breast. All that mattered was they were holding each other and they were touching. His head bent down so he could whisper.

"I will win. Don't worry, Brenda."

She blinked back tears. "I love you. I just want you to know that."

Chapter Eleven

ॐ

"Release my woman," Volder snarled.

"Not here," Zalk roared. "Back off, Volder. There will be no fighting in the chamber. We will take this outside to the arena."

Brenda turned her head, alarmed that Volder was so damn close. He was furious that Rever held her and the rage showed in his dark glower. Rever turned her in his arms and moved her out from between them. He released her but only to gently push her behind him, snarling at the other man.

Brenda peered around Rever's side at Volder, who looked ready to attack at any second. The guards moved once more, gripping Volder to push him away. Rever's tense body relaxed. His hand reached back, gripping Brenda's smaller one in his and he turned his head to look down at her.

"It will be fine. You are mine and I will win. I have everything to fight for."

Staring up into his eyes, she fought tears. "I don't want to lose you."

His blue eyes sparkled with amusement. "I am Argis and I will win."

Volder snarled. "Don't be so bold boasting your skills."

Brenda tore her gaze from Rever's, frowning at Volder. "Do you understand that I love him? Why fight for me when you know I will never be happy with you? I promise that we'd both be miserable if you forced me to be a part of your life. Don't you want a woman who wants you? I don't and I never will."

Fury made the man lunge forward but the guards grabbed him and hauled him back. Rever moved his body totally in front of Brenda's to protect her in case Volder broke free.

"Outside to the arena," Zalk roared.

The guards took a furious Volder out of the large room. The witnesses and the judge filed out next. All who remained in the chamber were Brenda, Rever, Coto and Rever's family.

"Much appreciated." Rever looked at his three brothers. "I owe you Ral, Vhon and Argernon."

Argernon snorted. "We are family. Be silent of vows." He carefully studied his brother. "Are you well enough to fight? Volder isn't a weak adversary. I have battled him in practice and he recovers very quickly. He is well trained so watch him very closely."

Rever gave a nod. "Understood." Rever's focus shifted to Coto, his expression tight with anger. "You —"

"Blame me," Hyvin Berrr suddenly gripped Rever's arm, turning him until they faced each other so son and father stared into each other's eyes. "I ordered Coto to tell me where you would take the human. He only did so because I asked. He would have died otherwise to keep silent. Volder was ready to have the entire crew of the *Drais* search the Outlander areas for you. I knew we could find a solution but you needed brought in alive to do so. Direct your rage at me. Coto was loyal."

Rever looked over his shoulder and his features softened when he met Coto's worried stare. "You protected my bound. Appreciated."

Coto gave a nod. "I am always loyal."

The expression on Rever's face softened more. "I knew it but I was angry."

"Understood." Coto hesitated. "If you fall I will challenge to protect your bound from Volder's wrath, with your permission. I know you feel very strongly for your human. Ral and Argernon are already bound so they may not offer." His gaze shifted to Vhon. "You definitely don't want to leave her in this one's care."

Vhon growled. "It was my plan to bring the other human here and I was the one to force the confession from Olt. It was my quick thinking that made this possible." His gaze slid to Rever. "You should be honored by letting me offer to challenge Volder for your bound if you fall."

Brenda stared at the tall men around her. "What is he talking about?"

Rever lowered his head to gaze at her. "If I don't win then Volder will claim you as his. Coto will challenge in the event of my death, winning no matter how well of a fighter Volder is because I will have worn him down. If I do fall, Coto will bound to you to protect you. Do you understand? He will cherish you in my place, Brenda."

"I will challenge for her first if you die," Vhon growled. "I am the one who made this challenge possible."

Brenda moved closer to Rever, not caring what the men around them thought of her touching him. Hot tears filled her eyes when she walked right into his chest and wrapped her arms around his thick body to cling to him. He could die and she didn't want him to. His arms encircled her waist tightly.

"Allow us moments alone," Rever said softly.

"I will challenge Volder if you fall," Vhon growled.

Hyvin Berrr snarled. "Enough. Rever will win the challenge. You are not mature enough to take on a bound."

Father and son were quietly arguing as they left. Rever inhaled a deep breath and then his hold on her loosened.

"Look at me, my bound."

She lifted her head, blinking back tears. "I don't want you to fight. I just want to go home with you. Why do you have to fight to the death? It's so damn stupid. I don't want to be with that man so why can't he just leave us alone?"

Rever's features softened. "It is about pride and warriors have too much of it at times. You belonged to his brother so he wants to keep you in the name of honor. Human females are also sexually stimulating to most Zorn males. It would be a great accomplishment for him to have one."

"But you love me. Volder has to know that you'll fight harder because of it."

"He knows that I do love you but he is very proud. Some males won't see reason." He reached up to cup her face. "I will win, Brenda. I have much to fight for because I have you."

She nodded. "I know you're a big badass. I get that. It doesn't mean I won't worry."

His black eyebrows arched. "Bad ass?" He stared down at her. "What is wrong with my backside?"

She couldn't help but smile. "It means you're one tough warrior. It's an Earth saying and it's a compliment. There's nothing wrong with your backside. You have the best ass I've ever seen."

A small smile curved his lips as he gave a nod. "I am tough."

"You are." She curled into his chest, loving the feel of his big body wrapped around her while he held her tightly.

"Don't worry, Brenda. I will take you home soon."

"I know you will." She feverishly hoped he would, unable to stand the thought of losing Rever.

"We will return to the house together."

That plan sounded heavenly to Brenda. Tina was gone now so Rever would come home to her every night after work and she could hold him whenever she wanted to, her body pressed tight to his larger frame every night, all night and she knew sleeping with Rever was heaven. He loved to cuddle with her head cushioned on his arm and her backside pressed to his front, spooning his body around hers, holding her tightly in his embrace.

"We must go," he said softly. "It is time."

She forced herself to release Rever when he gave her a nod, holding out his hand to her so she placed hers in his, walking together toward the doors where the guards waited outside. He kept hold of her until he had to let her go when they freed him from his chains and collar. Panic rose up inside her but then Rever met her eyes again.

"I will win."

"I know you will." She desperately hoped so, knowing she would go insane if she had to watch him die.

Brenda was stunned by the hundreds of Zorn males and females who stood silently in the street outside the building. A lot of them bowed their heads for long seconds. She turned to glance up at Rever. He looked proud and fierce as his gaze scanned the crowd. These were his people who had come to support him and their respect for him was obvious. Brenda didn't need anyone to tell her that was why they were all there.

Rever met Brenda's eyes. "You must stay back with the guards. This won't take long."

She watched helplessly as Rever strode away around the side of the building. She looked at the guards. "We're watching, right?"

One of them nodded. "In minutes they will let us in."

"In what?"

One of the guards educated her. "Both warriors will fight to the death in the arena behind that building. It was constructed for fighting out disputes when the need arose."

Her heart pounded and time seemed to crawl. One of the guards finally nodded. "Let us escort her to watch who the winner is."

Two men were going to fight to the death over Brenda and she was struggling to deal with it. The reality that Rever could really die was sinking in. Her heart squeezed painfully in her chest and she fought the urge to scream in frustration.

Why couldn't Volder let go of his stupid pride? What kind of idiot wants a woman who doesn't want him anyway? Her fear was quickly turning into anger at the big jerk.

The arena was an outdoor circle with a very tall, transparent wall around it, making it a large cage with no roof. It sat at a lower level than where people stood so that everyone could peer down at Volder and Rever in the circle area they stood in to fight each other.

Both men only wore pants. Volder's uniform and his boots had been taken from him while Rever had been given pants to put over his shorts. Brenda was led to the front so she could see the match better. She couldn't miss that the door exiting the arena was locked only feet away from where they placed her, trapping both men in the fighting area together. She also saw Rever's family standing close to her. Coto gave her a grim nod.

Brenda fixed her attention on Rever. He turned his head, scanning the crowd and finally found her when their gazes locked and held. His beautiful blue eyes narrowed at her and he gave her a nod before he turned away so she could stare at his back. Brenda wanted to scream out in frustration again, knowing this shouldn't be happening.

"Move," a woman yelled. "Get your big self out of the way. A pregnant woman is coming through."

Brenda turned her head and was astonished when she saw a long-haired blonde human walking toward her and beside her was a dark-haired human woman. The blonde was really pregnant, her rounded stomach showing she was at least six months along, and very noticeable as both women headed straight for Brenda. Large, mean-looking Zorn guards strode behind them, moving other Zorn away from the determined looking women.

The blonde walked right up to Brenda, giving her a wide smile. "I'm Ariel and I'm Ral's bound. He's Rever's brother." She waved a hand at the brunette. "This is Casey and she belongs to Argernon, Rever's other brother. We're family."

Ariel's tense looking eyes didn't reflect her smile. "How are you holding up? Your name is Brenda, right?"

"You're from Earth." Brenda was amazed by seeing two humans.

"Good guess," Casey said softly. "You poor thing, you're in shock. My Argernon filled me in on the details so I know you've had a rough time but we're here now. They wouldn't let us in the chambers for court because of some crap about women not being allowed inside during a judgment unless they were a witness or involved in the crime committed." She rolled her eyes. "They are old school here."

Ariel nodded. "For a technologically advanced civilization they can be downright mid-evil about some shit. We're here now and Rever is going to win so don't worry. Our guys are the best fighters."

Casey nodded. "They are stronger and faster than normal Zorn guys. That's why their father leads this planet as the ultimate ass kicker. Rever is going to take this Volder asshole down hard and fast."

Brenda fought tears. "Rever could die."

Ariel moved closer to put her arm around Brenda. "It's all right. We're here and you're not alone. Rever is not going to lose. Trust me when I tell you that the brothers are really mean fighters. I've seen Ral fight a lot, unfortunately. One guy is not going to be a problem for your Rever. I'd only be worried if like six or more were attacking him at once. One is a breeze compared."

Casey took up the space on Brenda's other side, gripping her loose hand hanging at her side, giving it a squeeze and holding on to it. "That's right. Our guys are major ass kickers. They grew up fighting each other for fun and you know how brothers are. You've got nothing to sweat."

Brenda felt a lot better now that she wasn't alone. She gratefully glanced at both women. "So we're family?"

"We're your sisters-in-law." Casey gave her a squeeze. "Hang in there. You'll laugh about this later. After you see him kick this guy's ass you'll feel silly about being so worried."

"That's right," Ariel said with a nod. "Our guys are winners."

A blare sounded, making Brenda jump but she wasn't alone. Casey and Ariel also startled.

"What was that?"

"I don't know," Casey admitted. "This is our first arena challenge that we've been to."

Ariel turned her head to look at the wall of guards behind them. "Jah? What is that alarm?"

The guard met Ariel's eyes. "It was the warning bell, Ariel. The fight will begin as soon as the challengers have finished proclaiming."

Casey frowned. "Did you catch that?" She was eyeing Ariel.

Ariel shrugged. "What in the hell is proclaiming?"

A horn sounded. Jah jerked his head in the direction of the arena. "Watch."

Casey moved in closer to Brenda. "It's going to be okay," she whispered.

Zalk climbed on something high so he was easily seen. "Now is the time for proclaiming. Speak now or it ends with the last breath."

Brenda saw Coto pushing his way forward in the direction of the older judge. She also saw Rever's younger brother Vhon move. He gripped the cage wall where a pole stood and climbed high, turning his head with a wide grin on his face.

"Zalk, if Rever falls I proclaim a challenge to Volder in his place for bounding rights."

Hyvin Berrr looked shocked and furious as he glared up at his son. Zalk wasn't fairing much better, looking stunned.

Coto froze for a few seconds but then turned his head, glaring up at Vhon. Vhon's grin spread wider. Brenda turned her head to look at Rever in the cage arena to see him frowning.

"Oh damn," Ariel sighed. "That little shit."

"Why did he do that?" Casey leaned over a little closer, almost bumping into Brenda. "What is going on? Coto was supposed to issue the second challenge thing."

Ariel shook her head. "Vhon is…" She closed her eyes and then snapped them open. "He's Vhon. He's kind of immature and well, he thinks with his lower region rather than with the brains in his head. It would be like handing your widow over to a super horny teenager." Her eyes slid to Brenda. "Rever will win so don't worry about it."

Casey chuckled. "Man, I wouldn't want to be you if Vhon did get his hands on you. If Argernon was any hornier I would need a wheelchair. You'd never survive the equivalent of Zorn's version of puberty."

Brenda stared at the brunette in shock.

"It was a joke," Casey assured her. "Rever's going to win."

Zalk nodded. "Proclaiming accepted and acknowledged." He turned to the arena. "Challenge begins now."

A roar instantly tore from the arena, which startled Brenda. She turned her attention back to the caged area just as Volder leapt at Rever. He moved just a heartbeat before Volder would have landed on him. Rever struck out with a strong arm, slamming it against Volder's chest. The other man staggered back, snarling. Rever snarled back as they circled each other.

"I can't watch," Brenda whispered but her eyes remained open.

"He'll win." Ariel hugged her side harder.

"He will," Casey echoed.

Brenda started to pray as the two men sprang at each other while fists were exchanged. Even from thirty some feet away she could hear the sound as knuckle met skin. She saw blood. The fist fight turned into kickboxing at times, both men lashing out at each other with powerful blows of their knees and feet when they weren't using fists.

Rever stumbled when Volder got in a lucky shot with his leg to the back of Rever's knee. Brenda moaned in terror for Rever when he went down but he rolled, getting up. Volder tried to attack him from the back. Rever looked as though he expected it, bending at his knees, he leapt up in the air, and flipped acrobat-style over the surprised Volder.

"Shit," Casey gasped. "He's in shape."

Volder spun around to face Rever when he landed behind him but it was too late. Rever threw a punch hitting Volder square in the jaw and sent him flying backward to land hard on the ground where he stayed, obviously stunned. He sat up after long seconds, shaking his head, blood running down his jaw, throat and bared chest, still looking dazed.

"Kill him," a male from the crowd roared.

More shout-outs followed that horrified Brenda as the Zorn people made vocally clear that they wanted to watch a man die. Rever didn't move though, waiting for Volder to get on his feet. Brenda saw Rever's lips move but the crowd was too loud to hear what he said. Volder looked pissed, shaking his head no in response, and stumbled to stand up. He advanced on Rever, who moved to meet him. Rever spun, his foot flying out, and nailed Volder hard in the front of his thigh.

Brenda almost screamed when she saw the gruesome sight of Volder's snapped leg. The bone came through the skin and Volder looked down in shock before he fell over. Blood shot upward from the horrific injury that his bone was showing from. The crowd went wild cheering.

Rever stood there for a few seconds looking furious while Volder lay there unmoving. One of Volder's shaking hands finally reached for the gushing wound to try to slow the bleeding but it was obvious from even afar that Volder was in bad shape and dying quickly as he bled out. Hot tears filled Brenda's horrified eyes as she watched Rever closing in to finish him off.

Dropping to his knes next to the fallen warrior, Rever's lips moved as he spoke to Volder. Rever suddenly bent over him, both hands grabbing hold of the bleeding leg and Rever roared out, his eyes going to Zalk. The crowd went silent. It was clear that Rever was gripping Volder's leg tightly to slow the bleeding, trying to save his opponent. Rever roared again.

Zalk nodded. "Send medical now that Volder has conceded. Argis Rever has won and is sparing Volder's life."

Brenda swayed on her feet in relief that Rever was alive. "Thank God."

"It's over," Ariel assured her. "He won and showed mercy to his opponent. Here comes medical now."

Brenda saw men and women in white as they rushed forward, the gate to the arena flung open to make it possible for the group of Zorn medical officers to work on Volder. Rever stood up and backed away but Brenda saw regret on his face. Blood soaked his hands, dripping from his fingers, and it was smeared on his body from the fight. He raised his head and their gazes locked.

Brenda moved, forcing both women to release her. No one tried to stop her as she approached the arena. The guard at the door moved aside for her as she walked for Rever, who stood there unmoving, watching her approach. She walked in front of him, staring up into his beautiful eyes when she stopped inches from his body.

"You won."

"I told you I would."

She didn't hesitate to throw herself at him to wrap her arms around his neck. He didn't hold her back but he did lower his jaw to kiss the top of her head. She noticed that

Rever kept both arms outstretched away from her and realized he was trying to not get her bloody.

"We will go home now."

She grinned. "We will go home together."

Rever smiled back. "I will bathe first. Then I am going to bound you to me again and again."

"I love a good plan."

He chuckled. "We will leave here now."

Outside the gate Rever's family waited. Rever paused when they reached the small group to look at each one of them. "You have my gratitude for forgiving the shame I caused."

Hyvin Berrr frowned at his son. "I raised you better."

Rever let his head lower, took a deep breath, and then his chin rose. He locked gazes with his father. "I love her."

The Zorn leader's look softened. "That is not what I meant. I raised you to know that I could never feel shame for what you do. You are a good warrior, a strong one who I am always proud of. Never feel gratitude for what you have earned from me. You caused no dishonor."

A grin split Rever's face. "Thank you, Father."

Vhon grinned. "I saved the day. I want a human woman now. Did I prove myself ready for bounding?"

Hyvin Berrr eyed his youngest son with a shake of his head. "No. I will however change your duties by giving you more responsibility. There is a ship to Earth that departs next moon cycle. I will let you go on a mission to reward you if you promise to not claim a human. You must prove worthy to bound first. It will be one of many missions to see how you do."

Vhon grinned. "Coolness! I'm so ready to get laid by some human chick. Bring on the jobs so I can earn one."

Ral frowned, his eyes narrowing slightly as his blue eyes slid to the short pregnant blonde tucked against his side. "Ariel?"

Ariel grinned up at him. "Sorry. He keeps asking me about human slang. He's such a sweetheart, how can I resist?"

The big warrior grinned at his bound. "I know all about not being able to resist someone. You are a bad influence."

Laughing, Ariel ran her hand over his stomach. "You never complain about my influences when I'm showing you how humans have sex in different ways."

He softly growled at her. "Let's go home. I am in need of a new lesson."

Licking her lips, Ariel smiled at him. "Let's go."

Argernon chuckled, winking at his bound. "Home sounds like a good idea. I think I need a nap, Casey."

Casey laughed. "You only need a nap when that's the code word for let's get naked and busy. Let's go." She winked back at him.

"I'll escort you home," Coto offered Rever. "It is the least I can do."

Brenda watched Rever's family say goodbye. The crowd was dispersing and medical carried an unconscious Volder away with his men following behind them. She wasn't his biggest fan but he was Valho's brother so she hoped that he would be all right. If it weren't for Valho, she never would have left Earth or met Rever.

She stayed within feet of Rever as he slowly walked down the street with her on one side of him and Coto on the other. They were going home.

Chapter Twelve
ဆာ

Brenda glanced around the bedroom with anticipation. Rever was in the shower and he wouldn't allow her in there with him, his reason was he didn't want Volder's blood on her. Ali was in the bedroom getting rid of all traces of Tina.

The grin on Ali's face was joyful. "You will be so happy here. I'm so glad that asshole is gone."

Chuckling, Brenda nodded. "Can I help?"

"No. I told you to hold still. I changed the bedding so her smell is gone." Ali grinned at her. "I will create a feast!"

Brenda walked over to the tall Zorn woman to give her a hug. "I'm glad to be here too."

Ali hugged her tight. "We are keeping you."

"Yes," Rever's deep voice spoke from the open bathroom door. "I am keeping her."

Brenda released Ali and turned to see that Rever was totally naked with only a small towel wrapped around his hips that did nothing to hide the fact that he was turned-on. Her gaze lowered to the bulge showing under the towel, lifting the front of it up noticeably. Her attention rose up his wet chest, taking in his muscled beauty, and her body instantly responded to how sexy he was. She wanted him badly.

Ali softly growled next to her. Brenda snapped her head to the side, staring up at the Zorn woman, unable to not recognize the lust in Ali's eyes. Brenda frowned.

"Ali?"

The woman tore her interested look away from Rever's body. "Yes?"

"I don't share and I will never tell him to touch another woman. I'm nothing like the asshole we just got rid of. Am I clear?"

A blush tinted Ali's features. "I was hopeful."

"Sorry. I love you to death but hands and tongue off my man."

Ali's shoulders sagged. "I understand. It is a human-alien thing."

"It is." Brenda bit her lip. "We're friends but I mean it."

Ali gave a nod. "I have males I can be with so I will leave yours alone, Brenda. I would never betray the trust of a friend."

All the tension left Brenda. "Why don't you leave Rever and I alone?"

A smile touched Ali's lips. "I will take my time preparing the feast while you both work up an appetite."

Ali left, closing the door firmly behind her. Brenda turned to face Rever, seeing that he had walked into the bedroom, his beautiful blue gaze fixed on her.

"I'm not Tina and I don't share. I know she didn't care if you let Ali touch you but I would."

Rever slowly moved forward. "I don't want Ali or any other woman. I just want you."

Relief swept through her. "Promise me?"

"I vow no other woman but you, my bound."

Reaching for her clothes, she started to strip. Rever's eyes narrowed as his breathing increased. He reached down, tearing away the towel, letting his thick cock spring free and upward now that it wasn't restrained by wet material. Brenda paused to stare, thinking *the guy is just too damn sexy for words*. Naked, she finally moved, walking toward him until she was within reach of him.

"I'm all yours, Rever."

He moved closer, his hands gripping her hips, lifting her. She wrapped around him without saying another word, meeting his hungry mouth with hers in a kiss that left her breathless and aching. She knew he was walking and felt when he lowered her onto the bed. His weight caged her down, pinning her tightly between soft mattress and hard male. His mouth left hers as their gazes locked.

"We will be happy," he softly growled in that sexy tone of his.

"I know."

"Are you ever sorry that I am not Valho? He talked you into leaving your world for this one."

"I never really knew him well, not like I know you, and I never loved him, Rever. I swear it was love at first sight when I laid eyes on you."

He smiled. "I felt like a warrior punched me in my belly the second my eyes met yours."

"So I made you feel sick?" She grinned, teasing him.

"My cock swelled so tight with the scent of you in my nose that I wanted to take you right there on the floor."

"I wish you had."

His smile slipped. "I wanted a human so badly that I bound to the wrong one too quickly. I knew I made a mistake immediately but it was already done and I am sorry for that. If I had not taken Tina from Earth, I could have bound to you so none of this happened and you never would have been in danger."

Reaching up, Brenda let her fingertips trace his jaw. "It ended up well and that's all that matters. We're together and no one can take us from each other, right?"

Chuckling, Rever gave a nod. "No one can separate us. Bounded couples are sacred on Zorn. Anyone who tries to take you from me will know immediate death."

She knew without a doubt that he'd kill for her. Her ex-husband wouldn't have even run to the damn grocery store for her if she begged but the man pinning her to his bed would do anything if she asked. She was so glad she'd left Earth, so happy that life was far behind her that she never even wanted to think back on it again. Her future was with this warrior, with Rever, here on Zorn.

"Make love to me."

"I will make love to you many times until we can't move."

She grinned. "Okay. I like that plan."

Brenda arched her eyebrows when Rever lifted off her body. "Where are you going?"

He went to his knees at the end of the bed on the floor, his large hands gripping her ankles, dragging her down the bed until her ass was on the edge. She relaxed her legs as he pushed them up and wide apart with a smile, knowing where this was leading. His gaze lowered from hers to stare at her exposed sex.

"I smell your need for me." His voice grew husky. "I love your scent."

"You make me wet just looking at you," she confessed.

His large hands caressed her thighs as his head dipped. Brenda closed her eyes when Rever's mouth found her clit, his tongue teased her, coaxing a moan from her lips. She loved his mouth on her. It felt amazing, the sensation sending raw pleasure throughout her body.

"Rever," she moaned his name.

His mouth sucked on her clit, tugging on the sensitive bud, vibrating as he growled in response to hearing her say his name. Inside her body, Brenda felt the inner walls of her pussy clenching, aching to be filled, knowing that in minutes she was going to come. Rever's relentless mouth and tongue teased her more and made her legs tremble. Her ass lifted off the bed to press tighter against his mouth and she knew heaven as her climax hit.

Tearing his mouth from her, Rever rose up quickly as his hands gripped her legs, to wrap them around his waist. She felt the press of his blunt cock against her pussy as he came down on her slowly. One of his hands got between their bodies to rub at her oversensitive clit gently. Both of them groaned loudly as he filled her slowly, breaching her tight entrance. He pushed into her deeper, seating himself fully inside her.

"Look at me, my bound," he rasped.

She couldn't resist gazing into his beautiful eyes. Rever stared back at her as he started to move in slow, deep thrusts of his hips. Brenda clawed the bed from the intense sensation of each movement he made that had ecstasy flowing through her. He was so thick that he hit about every nerve ending inside her and nothing had ever felt as good as Rever did to her.

His hips moved faster, causing even more pleasure to surge through their bodies, moans breaking from both of them as their breathing grew ragged. When Rever started to twist his hips a little, fucking her harder, Brenda bucked to meet each slam of his hips against hers. He angled his cock just a little more so he nailed her G-spot with every drive forward, his thick crown rubbed hard and fast against it, and he pressed down on her clit.

"Rever," she cried out.

"I'm here," he growled. "I have you. Feel me."

That was the problem. The sensations were too intense, too strong, and then Brenda was screaming out, jerking from the force of her orgasm over and over again, as he continued to move. Rever roared, his cock throbbing hard enough to feel as he came inside her, filling her up with his release.

Rever bent over her and braced his forearms next to her head. Brenda stared into his gorgeous blue eyes that glowed with love, a smile curving his full lips, and saw the same happiness she was experiencing reflected back at her.

"You are mine to love."

"I'm yours and I love you." She reached up, wrapping her arms around his neck. "Always, Rever."

His face lowered. "Always, my bound."

His kiss was tender, loving, and so sweet, loving him even more for being the kind of man who could be everything she needed. Brenda lifted her legs higher, wrapping them around his waist to cling to his body, never wanting to let him go. She broke the kiss, smiling at him.

Rever grinned at her. "I want you again."

She grinned back. "I always want you too."

"I want to do so many things to you. I want you on top of me and I want you to put me inside your mouth again. I want you bent over in front of me so I can take you from behind and I want—"

Brenda gave him a quick kiss, laughing, cutting him off.

"We can do it all. Lift off me so I can get up."

He moved, withdrawing from her body but he didn't look real happy to do what she asked. Brenda held back a laugh as she rolled over and went to her knees to crawl to the middle of his big bed. She flipped her hair out of the way, smiling at him over her shoulder on her hands and knees.

"Mount up, sexy. I'm making a mental list of things for us to do and this position is at the top of it."

Growling, Rever moved toward her in a heartbeat, his hands caressing her ass. "I hope this is a long list. I want you so much."

"It's so long that I figure it will take us twenty or so years just to reach the bottom of it. By then we'll have to start all over again because we'll be older and our memories probably won't be so good so we'll need reminded on what it was like by doing it again," she teased.

He chuckled, positioning his body against hers to slowly ease his cock into her body. Brenda's fingers clawed the bedding, a low moan leaving her mouth at the bliss of having him back inside her at a new angle.

"I'm on top next."

He growled from behind her. "You are the best thing that has ever come into my life, Brenda. You always tempt me in the best ways."

She pushed her ass back, forcing him in deeper, pleasure making her cry out. "Love me, Rever."

"Always." He started to move.

Also by Laurann Dohner

ဆ

eBooks:

Print Books:

About the Author

&

I'm a full time "in house supervisor" (Sounds *much* better than plain ol' housewife), mother, and writer. I'm addicted to carmel iced coffee, the occasional candy bar (or two), and trying to get at least five hours of sleep at night.

I love to write all kinds of stories. I think the best part about writing is the fact that real life is always uncertain, always tossing things at us that we have no control over, but when your write you can make sure there's always a happy ending. I *love* that about writing. I love it when I sit down at my computer desk and put on my headphones to listen to loud music to block out the world around me, so I can create worlds in front of me.

Laurann welcomes comments from readers. You can find her website and email address on her author bio page at www.ellorascave.com.

Tell Us What You Think

We appreciate hearing reader opinions about our books. You can email us at Comments@EllorasCave.com.

Why an electronic book?

We live in the Information Age—an exciting time in the history of human civilization, in which technology rules supreme and continues to progress in leaps and bounds every minute of every day. For a multitude of reasons, more and more avid literary fans are opting to purchase e-books instead of paper books. The question from those not yet initiated into the world of electronic reading is simply: *Why?*

1. *Price.* An electronic title at Ellora's Cave Publishing and Cerridwen Press runs anywhere from 40% to 75% less than the cover price of the exact same title in paperback format. Why? Basic mathematics and cost. It is less expensive to publish an e-book (no paper and printing, no warehousing and shipping) than it is to publish a paperback, so the savings are passed along to the consumer.

2. *Space.* Running out of room in your house for your books? That is one worry you will never have with electronic books. For a low one-time cost, you can purchase a handheld device specifically designed for e-reading. Many e-readers have large, convenient screens for viewing. Better yet, hundreds of titles can be stored within your new library—on a single microchip. There are a variety of e-readers from different manufacturers. You can also read e-books on your PC or laptop computer. (Please note that Ellora's Cave does not endorse any specific brands.

You can check our websites at www.ellorascave.com or www.cerridwenpress.com for information we make available to new consumers.)

3. *Mobility.* Because your new e-library consists of only a microchip within a small, easily transportable e-reader, your entire cache of books can be taken with you wherever you go.

4. *Personal Viewing Preferences.* Are the words you are currently reading too small? Too large? Too... ANNOYING? Paperback books cannot be modified according to personal preferences, but e-books can.

5. *Instant Gratification.* Is it the middle of the night and all the bookstores near you are closed? Are you tired of waiting days, sometimes weeks, for bookstores to ship the novels you bought? Ellora's Cave Publishing sells instantaneous downloads twenty-four hours a day, seven days a week, every day of the year. Our webstore is never closed. Our e-book delivery system is 100% automated, meaning your order is filled as soon as you pay for it.

Those are a few of the top reasons why electronic books are replacing paperbacks for many avid readers.

As always, Ellora's Cave and Cerridwen Press welcome your questions and comments. We invite you to email us at Comments@ellorascave.com or write to us directly at Ellora's Cave Publishing Inc., 1056 Home Avenue, Akron, OH 44310-3502.

MAKE EACH DAY MORE *EXCITING* WITH OUR

ELLORA'S
CAVEMEN
CALENDAR

☥ www.EllorasCave.com ☥

ELLORA'S CAVE
Romanticon

Annual convention
for women who
refuse to behave

www.JasmineJade.com/Romanticon
For additional info contact: conventions@ellorascave.com

Discover for yourself why readers can't get enough
of the multiple award-winning publisher
Ellora's Cave.

Whether you prefer e-books or paperbacks,
be sure to visit EC on the web at
www.ellorascave.com

for an erotic reading experience that will leave you
breathless.

Made in the USA
Lexington, KY
20 February 2015